THE **NAUGHTY** LIST

THE **NAUGHTY** LIST

suzanne young

razOr
bill

An Imprint of Penguin Group (USA) Inc.

The Naughty List

RAZORBILL

Published by the Penguin Group
Penguin Young Readers Group
345 Hudson Street, New York, New York 10014, U.S.A.
Penguin Group (USA) Inc., 375 Hudson Street, New York, New York 10014, U.S.A.
Penguin Group (Canada), 90 Eglinton Avenue East, Suite 700, Toronto, Ontario,
Canada M4P 2Y3 (a division of Pearson Penguin Canada Inc.)
Penguin Books Ltd, 80 Strand, London WC2R 0RL, England
Penguin Ireland, 25 St Stephen's Green, Dublin 2, Ireland
(a division of Penguin Books Ltd)
Penguin Group (Australia), 250 Camberwell Road, Camberwell, Victoria 3124,
Australia (a division of Pearson Australia Group Pty Ltd)
Penguin Books India Pvt Ltd, 11 Community Centre,
Panchsheel Park, New Delhi – 110 017, India
Penguin Group (NZ), 67 Apollo Drive, Rosedale, North Shore 0632, New Zealand
(a division of Pearson New Zealand Ltd.)
Penguin Books (South Africa) (Pty) Ltd, 24 Sturdee Avenue,
Rosebank, Johannesburg 2196, South Africa

Penguin Books Ltd, Registered Offices: 80 Strand, London WC2R 0RL, England

10 9 8 7 6 5 4 3 2 1

Copyright © 2010 Suzanne Young

Library of Congress Cataloging-in-Publication Data
Young, Suzanne.
p. cm.
Summary: Head cheerleader Tessa runs the ultra-secret SOS,
or Society of Smitten Kittens, that spies on her fellow-students'
cheating boyfriends, until her own boyfriend is implicated.
ISBN 9781595142788
[1. Dating (Social customs)--Fiction. 2. Interpersonal relations--Fiction. 3. Cheerleading--Fiction.
4. High schools--Fiction. 5. Schools--Fiction. 6. Honesty--Fiction.] I. Title.
PZ7.Y887 Nau 2010
[Fic] 22

2009021094

Printed in the United States of America

In loving memory of my grandmother,
Josephine Parzych.

SOS
~~POSSIBLE CHEATER ROSTER~~

The Naughty List!

UPDATED:

~~Adler, Josh~~—*caught*

Bryant, Michael—*under investigation*

~~Bullard, Robert~~—*caught*

~~Chandler, Cash~~—*caught*

~~Dougherty, Phillip~~—*caught*

Hanlon, Harley—*under investigation*

~~Hanrick, Bradley~~—*caught*

~~Jackson, Cade~~—*caught*

Letterman, Noah—*under investigation*

~~Mill, Michael~~—*totally caught!*

~~Naples, North~~—*caught*

Raffule, Richard—*under investigation*

~~Reen, Andrew~~—*caught*

~~Sanders, Sage~~—*caught*

SOS
CHEATER INCIDENT REPORT

CASE: 042
CLIENT: Natalie Snyder
SUBJECT: Dwayne Brooks
FINDINGS: At approximately 9:15 p.m. on January 27, Mr. Brooks was observed engaging in a make-out session with a girl other than the client. The incident took place in the back row of the Regal Cinemas, theater 2. The movie was an ultra-lame romantic comedy.

Enclosed are the photos documenting the incident. There are three photos of Mr. Brooks in a lip-lock, one at the concession stand, where he bought his female companion Twizzlers, and two others, which were taken while the pair were parked in front of the female's house. Note that the final photo confirms third base.

We trust that this report will remain confidential as some of the information contained within could compromise our top-secret status.

SOS is sorry for your loss, and we offer our deepest sympathies. We hope that we will not have to assist you again in the future, but please keep us in mind for referrals.

Keep smiling,

SOS
Text: 555-0101
Exposing Cheaters for Over Two Years

CHAPTER ONE

SIGH. A PADLOCK? WHO PADLOCKED THEIR GATES in this neighborhood? This was Brinkerhoff Point—one of the nicest areas in the entire state of Washington! "Bobby pin," I whispered, exhausted from climbing the hill with a backpack full of gear. I'd had to park nearly three blocks away.

"Oops," Kira said, biting her well-glossed lip. "I wore my hair down tonight." I narrowed my eyes at her as she fluffed her blond curls. "Sorry, Tess. I wanted to look good in case we bumped into Darren."

"At two in the morning?"

She shrugged, scrunching her nose. Kira was sweet, even when she forgot the necessary break-in equipment. I slid the heavy backpack off my shoulders, dropped it onto the grass, and squatted.

The well-manicured side yard provided perfect cover— high bushes, dark corners, and no motion detectors. Score. As I unzipped the front pocket, I glanced at the full moon, noting that it lit up the entire sky. It was time to kick this mission into high gear. Getting caught breaking into Michael Garnett's house would be a horrible inconvenience. If we were in a holding cell, we'd totally miss cheerleading practice!

"Holy cannoli, K! What did you pack?" There was so much stuff in the bag that the pen I was searching for was lost in a sea of night vision cameras, flashlights, GPS trackers, and . . . *panties*? "Ew!" I yanked out my hand.

She giggled. "There they are!"

"Kira, a Smitten Kitten doesn't carry her panties around in a backpack. She wears them under her clothes."

There was a rustling in the backyard on the other side of the fence, and my breath stopped. Mashed potatoes and gravy! Was someone awake?

"Move," I whispered, putting my arm out to back us slowly away across the grass. Seconds passed, and the noise settled into the chirping of crickets. I tried to breathe, my chest heaving under my one-piece black kitten suit. It wasn't as tight as Kira's ensemble, but it was still snug and totally flattering. Especially since I'd been working out more—lycra wasn't very forgiving. Suddenly, a gray cat jumped up and balanced on the top of the wooden gate, looking us over. It meowed once and then strolled across the length of the fence before jumping into the neighbor's yard. I exhaled.

"Aw . . ." Kira said, quietly clapping. "I love kitties."

I shook my head and got down on my knees in the damp grass to go through the items Kira had prepped for this mission. Obviously, she'd missed the memo that required all assignments to be stocked with a lock pick (or bobby pin). Oh, well, at least she had panties this time.

When I finally found the pen, I plucked off the cap and walked up to the padlock, twisting the plastic carefully inside it.

Click.

"Get the bag," I whispered. "I'll need the webcam."

Michael Garnett had been accused of cheating on his girlfriend,

Caitlyn, with someone he'd met on MySpace. Unfortunately, he was constantly changing his password, so that every time I cracked his code, he'd made a new one. If I didn't know any better, I'd say he was on to SOS. But I did know better. Nobody outwitted the Society of Smitten Kittens. We were seriously stealth.

I pushed open the heavy wood gate, and Kira followed me as we made our way to the back of his enormous brick house. Michael's bedroom was on the first floor, and that was a good thing. I was not in the mood to scale a wall tonight.

We paused in front of his window and ducked down, peeking between the slots of his blinds. Only guys forgot to close their blinds. The room was dark, but his computer's screen saver tossed out enough light so that I could see Michael's husky figure, turned away from me in the bed.

Thankfully, Leona had come by earlier in the week and mapped the place out. Michael's computer was right next to the window, which made this assignment possible. Otherwise, I would have never taken the chance on breaking in. Or at least, breaking in while he was home.

Quietly and carefully, I slid open the pane and raised the blinds. Perfect. Not a sound. I looked back at Kira, and she gave a dimpled smile and a big thumbs-up. I appreciated her support.

I leaned in the window, putting my weight on my stomach as I pulled myself through. Silently, I eased my sneakers onto the carpet and let my eyes adjust to the darkness.

Michael was a safe distance away, snoring softly. Ick. His room smelled like sweaty socks and Axe body spray. I twitched my nose.

Stretching my arm back through the window, I held out my hand for the webcam. It was an exact replica of the one balanced on Michael's computer, totally on sale at spytime.com! Leona had ordered new equipment that could send a direct feed to the SOS database. She was great at more than high kicks and herkies. She was a computer whiz.

Carefully, I removed the wires and clipped the new cam on the computer frame. Then I leaned forward over Michael's desk and looked into the lens, waiting.

"Got the signal," Kira whispered from outside. I smiled and winked at the camera.

As I straightened up, I noticed Michael's cell phone plugged in and resting on the side table next to a box of tissues. Hm. Cautiously, I made my way toward it.

Just then, Michael moaned, and the bedsprings creaked as he turned over. I dropped to my stomach on the carpeted floor. I was about to get busted! If my boyfriend found out I was sneaking around in another guy's room, he would kill me!

A few feet away, I heard squeaks and the sound of sheets rustling. Was he getting up? Instinctively, I tucked my arms at my sides and rolled under his bed, only a second before I saw his bare feet hit the ground. I swallowed hard, trying to keep my breathing quiet as I watched him walk forward, scratching at his flannel-pajamaed rear. Gross.

It felt like a bazillion seconds, but finally, he opened his bedroom door and walked out into a brightly lit hallway. I needed to escape.

Quickly, I scrambled out from under the bed and pushed aside Michael's leather desk chair as I made for the window. I paused, mid-getaway, and turned back. I wanted that sim card from his phone. I moved fast.

My polished fingers shook as I quickly slid off the metal back cover and removed the battery. From outside the room, I heard a toilet flush. Cranberry juice cocktail! I had to go.

I plucked out the card and snapped the battery case shut. There was the soft creak of a door hinge, and I dropped the phone and dashed to the window. I dove and had barely gotten my sneakered heel through when the bedroom door opened. I front-flipped and fell into the grass, Lycra-covered rear first, and stared up into Kira's terrified expression.

I put my finger to my lips and motioned for her to get to the gate. Still lying on my back, I opened my palm. Sim card.

Strawberry smoothie.

Kira had calmed down by the time we reached my car. She wasn't very good at handling stress sometimes. She suffered from post-traumatic SOS disorder. In fact, after our last mission at the Regal Cinemas, Kira had a panic attack and nearly choked on a Twizzler.

"Oh," she said as she buckled her seat belt. "At practice Leona wants to talk about a name change. Everyone is still calling us the Sex Kittens, and she thinks it's demeaning." Kira breathed on the passenger window and then traced *K* ❤ *D* into it.

I sighed. We'd had this conversation before. "I understand, but just because we've agreed to stop using the name doesn't mean the rival schools will. We cheer for the Wildcats, K. It makes sense that with our good looks, they'd come up with Sex Kittens. I give them credit for being clever."

Truth was, I *did* think the name was offensive, which was why I took it upon myself to call us the *Smitten* Kittens whenever possible. It had a much better connotation. And besides, it rhymed!

Still, most of the boys at school called us the Sex Kittens, including my boyfriend. Technically, our name was the Society of Smitten Kittens (SOS), only . . . without the K. Acronyms were ridiculously hard! Plus SOS sounded way more official than SOSK.

"You're right," Kira said, adjusting the aim on the heater vents. "And honestly, I don't mind being a Sex Kitten. It's way better than being a Cougar, right?" We both laughed. The rival squad at Templeton High was totally lame.

Even though we occasionally helped out the girls at other schools, we tried not to go too far out of our district. It was harder to get accurate information, and it made carpooling difficult. But we prided ourselves on being an equal opportunity operation.

When my car heated up, I shifted into gear and began driving toward Kira's apartment complex. She lived in the Marshall District—an older section of town on the other side of the freeway. It was mostly duplexes and mom-and-pop shops, but it was closer to the mall, which Kira was stoked about. Especially since she didn't have a car.

"Just remember," I said as I stopped at a red light. "If we act like the name bothers us, they'll only use it more. What's the Smitten Kitten motto?"

"Never let them see you sweat," she announced, looking proud to have remembered this time.

"Exactly. Because Kittens. Don't. Sweat."

I bit on my lip as the light changed to green. I wanted to believe those words, but sometimes in this business, perspiration was unavoidable. I'd known back when we'd first started that SOS would be a hard gig. Harder than a double-flip basket catch.

It was two years ago when our cheerleading captain, Mary Rudick, had been cheated on. Her boyfriend, Kyle, had been the Wildcats' power forward and an all-around nice guy, or so we'd thought. Turns out he'd been running a screen.

At a playoff game, a girl showed up—obviously from a rival school because she seriously lacked school spirit—and stomped down the bleachers in heels during halftime. We were all waiting on the sidelines for our signal to go out and cheer when the girl came over, not even dressed in our colors. She asked Mary if she was still dating Kyle, and Mary, always polite, said that she was indeed his girlfriend.

But instead of congratulating her, the girl laughed right in Mary's face! She said that for the past year, Kyle had been seeing *her* and that Mary needed to back off. Turns out, Kyle had been sleeping with both of them!

As the girl spoke, Mary had just stood there, completely silent. I felt like I had to do something to stop the self-esteem assault, so with emergency captain authority, I'd told the girl to leave. *Very sternly.* She gave a little smirk before shoulder bumping me and exiting the gymnasium.

The buzzer had sounded, signaling time for our halftime cheer, but Mary didn't move. Her pom-poms dropped to the wood floor with a double thwack. My heart broke. And then my adrenaline kicked in.

I marched out onto center court, soon followed by the others. I cheered my stuffing out. The power was amazing as the crowd reacted to my every word. I remember watching the sidelines as Mary stumbled back a few steps and sat in a folding chair, staring straight ahead, her dark eyes glassy with tears. I cheered louder.

By the end of the game, I had nearly lost my voice, and Mary wasn't speaking. She left before Kyle could find her, but I saw that he knew. He offered me his signature crooked smile, but I just turned and stormed out.

The next day, Mary pulled all the squad into a meeting and discussed starting a club—one that caught cheaters. After careful observation, we noticed that our school had an abnormally high cheater-to-girlfriend ratio. I theorized that maybe it had something to do with the rainy weather.

So with the help of the internet, some spy books, and a few James Bond flicks, we set out on our first mission. It took us a while to get the right balance between investigating and cheering, but after a few false starts, we got it to stick. Mary drafted the official handbook, and ever since then, all Smitten Kittens doubled as official cheater catchers.

After she graduated, Mary deemed that I had more spirit than anyone she'd ever encountered, so she turned SOS over to me. I took my role as leader very seriously. I'd never let another girl suffer because of her boyfriend's extracurricular activities. There'd never be another Mary Rudick.

I smiled to myself. Luckily, I didn't have to worry about *Aiden* cheating. He was my perfect guy, practically a life-size boyfriend trophy. Oh, so cute and—

"Hey," Kira said, pointing out the windshield. "You just passed my place."

"Oops." I shook my ponytailed head as I slowed my car and pulled to the curb a few buildings down. "I'm sorry. I was just thinking about something."

"Or some*one*." Kira made kissing noises and rubbed at her shoulders in a fake make out.

I laughed but then caught sight of the dashboard clock and groaned. Even though it was twenty minutes fast (so I'd never be late), it read three in the morning. "K?" I asked. "Do you mind if I reschedule practice until after school? I'm not sure I can jump as high as I need to this morning."

"No prob. I'll e-mail the girls when I get in." She took out her cell and adjusted her calendar. Then she grinned, looking sideways at me. "I'm sure Aiden will appreciate a little more quality time with you anyway."

I swatted her shoulder. "Be quiet. Aiden gets plenty from me." And he did. Except for the truth about where I'd been spending my nights. I swallowed hard and took the sim card from my cup holder and handed it to Kira. "Track down all the numbers on this," I said. "I want the names of everyone Michael has been calling other than Caitlyn. Full report tomorrow."

"On it, Tess."

"And let me know what you see on the webcam." She saluted me, and I slipped the car into reverse until I was in front of her building entryway. After all, it was three in the morning.

"See you at school," she said happily as she climbed out. She loved when I trusted her with evidence.

I watched her blond curls flop around on her shoulders as she jogged to the front gate of her complex. She waved one last time and I waved back, mostly to encourage her. But the minute she was gone, my smile faded.

Just once, I wanted *not* to confirm a cheat, to find at least one innocent guy. But so far, SOS subjects had been found guilty hundred percent of the time. It was tragic. And it was seriously impeding my perk.

I sighed and shifted my car into gear before pulling onto the street, headed for my home in Murray Hills. With a quick check at my reflection, I straightened my frown and tried to look positive.

It was possible. It was possible to find at least one innocent suspect. I was sure of it.

SOS
THE OFFICIAL HANDBOOK

UPDATED:

OUR MISSION STATEMENT: The mission of SOS (the Society of Smitten Kittens) is to make a positive difference in the dating lives of the girls at Washington High—primarily through investigation, client confidentiality, and inspirational cheer sets—all the while building the self-esteem, individuality, and confidence of the female population by providing a high standard of leadership, competence, and fabulous accessorizing.

SMITTEN KITTEN CODE OF CONDUCT:

- Never be seen at the location of an investigation. Being covert means being invisible.
- Never leave a Smitten Kitten behind. When faced with exposure, use the predetermined escape routes and stay in formation.
- Always be upbeat and positive. School spirit is essential to success.
- Refrain from using any profane language. Smitten Kittens never cuss.
- Be on time for all practices, games, and SOS meetings and missions.
- Do not engage in any dating activities with a suspect. Making out with a suspect is bad form.
- Dress appropriately for all games and missions. Cheer

skirts for games, spandex for practice, and black, drab outfits for missions.

° Although a Smitten Kitten is often privy to detailed encounters of the cheating variety, she must always maintain her class in and out of school. Never speak to anyone outside of SOS about the missions. If needed, an SOS-approved counselor can help with post-traumatic-SOS-disorder-related issues.

THE LAWS:

° The Cheat—An official cheat requires the subject to be engaged in romantic or sexual activity with a person other than the client. These offenses include, but are not limited to, hand-holding, kissing, dirty talk, or any of the four bases.

° Double Jeopardy—We will never investigate the same subject twice for the same cheat. Once cleared or convicted, the subject is free to continue his inappropriate lifestyle without our supervision.

° Evidence—Each subject is innocent until proven cheating. To confirm the crime, more than one form of evidence must be provided to the client. This can include photos, audio or video surveillance, e-mails, eyewitness accounts, recovered items with fingerprints or DNA, or admission of guilt. Instincts and bad reputations do not count as evidence.

° Interference—Never interfere with a cheat in progress. Although it may be difficult to witness these crimes of passion, it's the SOS responsibility to investigate without bias.

° Confidentiality—It is key to every mission to maintain the secrecy of the client and the SOS organization. Never engage a client or subject directly with collected evidence. All communication must be anonymous.

DISCIPLINE: If a Smitten Kitten is caught breaking these rules, an official disciplinary form will be sent. The infractions could result in
° Verbal or written warnings
° Suspension of assignment
° Loss of cheer time
° Dismissal

PAYMENT AND EQUIPMENT: SOS is a nonprofit organization. There is no charge for our services, and all proceeds from donations go directly toward equipment and other essential supplies, like uniforms. Only the president and treasurer have access to these funds.

RESPONSIBILITIES: Smitten Kittens are expected to keep a cheerful attitude at all times. The SOS reputation is dependent on the squad's conduct along with our success on missions.

All Smitten Kittens are responsible for learning cheers, stunts, lock picking, wall scaling, equipment handling and maintenance, and herkies.

Never let them see you sweat! Go, Smitten Kittens!

CHAPTER TWO

I CHECKED TO MAKE SURE THE DOUBLE DOORS OF
the gymnasium were shut before crossing the wood floor to pause
in front of my squad.

"Kitten call to order," I said, clapping. The Smitten Kittens
were gathered on the front wooden bleacher, packing up their cheer
gear. We'd just finished practice, and I was sweaty and exhausted.
But we had business to attend to.

"I need the double scoop. What's the status report?" I asked
Kira, readjusting my ponytail.

"There's over two hundred numbers on the sim card," she said,
rolling her eyes. "Who would have thought Michael Garnett had so
many friends? He's such a tool."

"Kira," I scolded. "Be objective."

"Sorry." She shrugged apologetically and then reached into her
backpack to pull out a manila folder, setting it on her lap. "I've
printed out the names, and I'm doing a run-through now. I'll need
another day."

"Great job, K. I'm totally impressed."

Leona groaned from the end of the bleacher, and Kira glanced
over at her, beaming. Leona rolled her eyes.

"Be nice," I mouthed to Leona. "Now, what about the webcam?"
She adjusted her glasses and looked down, checking her phone for

the feed. "Nada. But that's to be expected, Tess. He seems like a night perv."

I tsked. The squad had been very judgmental lately. I blamed the fact that we'd caught several of their boyfriends cheating on them in the past three months. Poor things. It was tragic, really.

"I have something," Izzie announced, twisting a red strand of her hair around a pen.

I nodded to her, wondering if she'd found a crucial piece of evidence in Michael's MySpace account. We would need at least two forms of cheater tracks to confirm the crime.

Izzie pulled her ruby red lips into a smile and stood up. "Okay, so I was at the mall yesterday, and I saw this *totally* cute maroon warm-up suit that would be perfect for non-game days!" She bounced on her heels with excitement, eagerly waiting for our response.

I stared at her. The other girls on the squad stopped what they were doing to turn to her. She stayed standing for a minute and then widened her eyes before sitting down on the bleacher. She shrugged and mumbled, "And I found dirty MySpace messages that were placed to Lisa Belgium. She and Michael have been sleeping together for, like, two months."

"Nice!" Leona called, clapping. "Now we just need the sim card info or the webcam images, and he's busted! Get me all the files so I can draft the report and submit it for Tessa's approval."

The girls started congratulating each other, happy to have uncovered another cheater, but I felt my face drain of color. Even though I'd known from the beginning that we'd probably catch Michael doing *something*, I'd still hoped that the accusation wasn't true. I always did.

But nothing ever changed. One hundred percent guilty. Just like always.

I wrapped my arms around myself and walked over to the bleachers to pick up my cheerleading gear. My school spirit was compromised.

"Meeting adjourned," I said quietly, and headed for the double doors of the gymnasium. I needed Aiden. He always knew how to cheer me up.

I pushed back into my soft, pink pillows, staring at the lean muscles of Aiden's arm as he held my leg. "You should have been there," I said, reaching down to run my fingers over his skin. "Izzie caught me in the hall and was like—"

"Tessa," Aiden said, getting a better position on the edge of my bed. "Will you stop wiggling?"

"Oh, sorry. But I just think—"

"I know, baby. You're always thinking. Can I please finish?" He smiled, his green eyes sparkling deviously.

"Okay."

He exhaled and picked my foot back up, using the brush of the pink passion nail polish to go over my pinky toe. It might seem odd that my boyfriend loved to paint my toenails, but I thought it was sweet. After two years, he'd actually gotten really good at it. Way better than I was. And why pay some stranger to torture me with a pedicure every few weeks when Aiden liked to do it as foreplay? He was so cute like that.

"Finished," he said, blowing on my foot before laying it in his lap. He closed the bottle and set it on my rosewood side table. Then he leaned over to kiss my ankle. When his warm mouth touched my skin, a shiver ran up my leg.

"Thanks." I licked my lips. He was absolutely, mind-blowingly adorable.

His eyes narrowed as he kissed lightly at my shin, then my knee. Even in the gloomy November weather, his skin was tan. Set that against his green eyes and tousled blond hair, and the boy was pure eye candy. But he never noticed when other girls checked him out. He never noticed anyone but me.

When we'd started dating, he was already super-tall and sort of awkward. Some of the older girls on the squad even thought he was beneath me, totally average. But I knew, even back before his increasingly sexy biceps, that Aiden would be more than the star of the basketball team. He was perfect for me. We were, well, partners. Neither one of us ruled the other. It was a give-and-take. We—

"Mm . . ." I loved when he caressed my leg like that. I closed my eyes, adjusting my position and staring at my ceiling fan as it swirled. My nail polish would undoubtedly be ruined in a few minutes. It always got ruined. Luckily, I wore sneakers 95 percent of the time.

Aiden's hands slid up, pausing on my hips. I nestled back into my fluffy white comforter. My parents wouldn't be home for hours. One of the perks of having musical parents was that their nights were spent in lounges, leaving tons of free time for Aiden . . . or SOS. Either way, it was still way better than having a mom that worked for H&R Block—poor Aiden.

"Can you leave this on?" he mumbled into my thigh, touching the hem of my skirt.

I laughed, reaching down to push his hands away. "I'm not wearing my uniform so you can act out some boyhood fantasy yet again."

"Please? It's so fucking hot."

"Aiden, don't talk like that."

"Sorry, baby. It's so freaking hot."

He knew I'd agree. I always did. I mean, there was a reason I kept three extra maroon and gray skirts in my closet, even if this one was my favorite. My boyfriend could be very persuasive.

"Afterward, I get to talk about whatever I want," I said. Aiden usually preferred a nap to listening to my latest cheerleading drama, but this was important! Izzie had a new cheer!

The bed shifted as Aiden crawled up and stretched his long body next to mine, leaning over to kiss my neck. "Mm-hm."

"And then you have to repaint my nails."

"Okay."

"And—"

He pressed his mouth to mine. He knew how to shut me up.

"Aiden," I whispered, twisting his hair with my finger.

"What?" he mumbled. He'd been lying facedown on the bed, totally passed out.

"You have to go home. Your mom's going to freak." I leaned down and kissed his earlobe. It was close to ten, and he'd been at my house since I'd gotten home from practice.

"Can't I stay here?"

He knew he couldn't, but it didn't stop him from asking every time—not that my parents would care. They adored him. In fact, my father called him "son." My parents even decorated signs to hold up at the games. Signs that said things like, "The Wildcats Can't Be Caged" or "Growl Till It Hurts." Yes. They were *those* people.

"Your mother is going to call here in, like, five minutes." I really didn't want him to go. I lifted his arm and snuggled up next to him, breathing his natural, athletic scent. Even though the physicality of our relationship was a recent development, it was quickly becoming my favorite part. *Especially* when we got to do this afterward. I held him a little tighter.

"Mm," he said sleepily, turning to wrap his other arm around me. "But I like it better at your house."

I stared at him. He was so handsome. His eyes were closed as his face rested on the pillow, but there was the hint of a smile on his lips. He knew I was watching him.

"What?" he whispered, his eyes still shut.

"I just love you."

"I know you do, baby." He opened one eye to look at me. "Give me a kiss."

Leaning over, I pecked his lips.

"And another," he breathed. I giggled.

The phone rang and we paused, still connected at the mouth.

"Told you," I mumbled into his lips.

He groaned, reaching up to rest his palm on my cheek. Aiden adored me. He absolutely worshipped me. But he still had to go home. I was pretty sure his mother couldn't stand me. She might have been suffering from a case of cheerleader envy.

I kissed him again quickly and sat up. He rolled onto his back, grabbing his T-shirt from the side table. He slid it over his head as the phone rang its third warning call. I raised one eyebrow at him.

"Tell her I left five minutes ago?" he asked, tilting his head.

I nodded and scooted down the bed. She wouldn't believe me; I always told her the five-minute story. Walking into the hallway, I grabbed the cordless off the wall and pressed it to my ear. Out of the corner of my eye, I saw Aiden streak by, dashing to the door. Even though he pretended not to be, I knew he was terrified of his mother. I would be too.

"Hello?" I asked in my sweetest voice.

"Tessa?"

It was Kira, and she sounded awful—totally choked up.

I jetted my glance toward the direction Aiden ran, but I heard the front door close, signaling his hasty exit. He'd be away at college next year, but we'd still be strawberry smoothie. Washington State University wasn't all that far, and with a dorm room in his immediate future, there would be sleepovers. My senior year was going to rock.

"Are you there?" Kira whimpered.

Oh, right. "What's wrong, K? And why are you calling on my house phone?"

"Because I'm a mess! He cheated!"

My stomach flipped. "Who?"

"*Darren* cheated."

"Cheated, like how? At Scrabble?"

"No!" She sniffled back some thick-sounding snot. I cringed. "Tessa, my boyfriend cheated on me! And we didn't know about it!"

My eyes widened. Wait, that wasn't possible. We knew about every cheater. The SOS team was constantly updating the possible cheater roster (or as I liked to call it, the Naughty List), and Darren was definitely *not* on it. No one got by the Society of Smitten Kittens. Especially not one of our boyfriends!

"Who's the girl?" I asked, tapping my bare foot on the carpet.

"Charlie Meyers."

"Whoa. His ex-girlfriend?" This was a disturbing development. It should have been obvious because guys always cheated with their exes. It was practically a given.

"That's the one." Her voice became little more than a high-pitched dog whistle. I closed one eye and clenched my teeth as I listened.

She tried to regain her composure. "Kara's cousin's girlfriend saw them in the parking lot of the Windmill hotel—"

"Ew. The one where you pay by the hour?" My mouth flooded with a familiar metallic taste: adrenaline.

"I know!" Her sounds came out in a guttural moan. "And it wasn't even a Sheraton! I totally thought Darren had better taste than that!"

Now I was seriously PO'd. Darren was Aiden's best friend and the power forward of the Wildcats. Next to Aiden, he was our leading scorer. Well, next to Aiden, he was our only scorer. That deserved *R-E-S-P-E-C-T.*

"What are we going to do?" she whined. "Every guy we've investigated has been guilty. Every one! And look at *us.* None of us even have boyfriends anymore." She sniffled. "We've become a squad of widows."

"Widows are the spouses of people who have died, K."

She gasped. "My word! That is so sad!"

Even though I felt awful for Kira, she was wrong. One of us did still have a boyfriend. Me.

"Wait." She sighed. "Never mind, you have Aiden. You're the only Smitten Kitten that hasn't been cheated on."

Somehow that thought made me uncomfortable.

"Oh, no!" she said loud enough to make me jump. "I won't be able to go to prom!"

Kira dissolved into hysterical sobs. As I tried to soothe her, I spun around, still clad in a slightly wrinkled cheerleading skirt. The heater kicked on, and when I felt the warm breeze on my legs, I looked down.

Smeared nail polish. Aiden. Cheaters. Fudge ripple! Something was wrong.

"I'll call you back," I said, clicking off the phone. Darren was a Wildcat, and my boyfriend was his captain. That made him Aiden's responsibility. He needed to rein in this mess or I would get cheeredieval on his rear.

I set the phone back on the wall and marched to my room. Aiden's mom would be less than thrilled to see me tonight, so I'd have to climb up the latticework to his room. Again.

I sighed. Why was everything getting so complicated? Couldn't I just cheer, come home, hook up with my boyfriend, and go to sleep?

Searching through my closet, I looked past the rows of mission-specific attire—one-piece bodysuits, spandex running pants, utility belts with climbing gear, and tons of hats and scarves.

Aha! There, near the back, was the only clean black shirt I had that wasn't for SOS. My mother had gotten it for me when she was in her bohemian rhapsody phase. It was seriously drab. It took most of my willpower to not pair it with the cute metallic leggings I'd just bought and instead choose dark jeans. I wouldn't want Aiden's mom to spot me sneaking in. That certainly wouldn't help her negative attitude.

I glanced in my full-length mirror. Great. I looked like a ninja. What I wouldn't do for my squad, for girls everywhere.

I tied my dark strands into a still-cute, yet casual high knot and contemplated using black eyeliner to ring my eyes. Never mind, there was no need to go overboard. I grabbed my oversized purse, tossing its strap onto my shoulder as I headed to the doorway.

Aiden would be excited to see me, at least. And I did still need him to fix my toenails, even though I had a feeling we'd just get carried away again. I glanced in my purse quickly and smiled when I spied my extra bottle of ruby red polish.

A Smitten Kitten was always prepared.

I paused under Aiden's window, looking from the large porch in the front to his darkened pane, charting my usual course. There was latticework with interwoven vines attached to the white siding, and amazingly enough, it wouldn't be the first lattice I'd climbed this week.

When we'd investigated Peter Corning on Tuesday, I'd had to shimmy across his cedar roof to get a picture of him cheating. He and his female accomplice were totally getting it on in his parents' room! Gross.

His girlfriend, Marissa, was so ticked when she found out, she'd given him a bloody lip in the middle of homeroom! It was quite a scene—swearing, punching, and groin kicking.

Sheesh. Peter would freak if he knew how Marissa had found out about his cheating. So far, none of the guys knew SOS existed—our clients were great at keeping the secret. Even better, *nobody* outside of the Smitten Kittens knew our true identities. And we planned to keep it that way.

My sneaker fit perfectly in between the slots of the wooden grid as I climbed. My pulse was racing. Heights weren't my thing. Well, not unless I had a good solid base beneath me, and this latticework was nowhere near as dependable as my girls. They would never drop me.

Aiden's window was half open, and I smiled. I figured it would be, since I snuck in to see him about twice per week. It would have been quite an inconvenience if I had to pick the lock every time. I pushed the cold glass up all the way before crawling in.

"Hey," I whispered as I slid my legs over the sill. Aiden's

bedroom was lined with trophies and ribbons dating back to elementary school. My sweetie had even earned a merit badge from Boy Scouts for knot tying. But what I loved most was that his room smelled like him: athletic, sexy, and comforting. His sheets rustled as he shifted in the bed.

"Baby?" He sounded sleepy. Aiden sat up and clicked on his side table lamp, lighting up the room. I noticed that the tracksuit he'd been wearing earlier was tossed on the wood floor. It made me wonder what exactly he was wearing under his sheets. I licked my lips.

Aiden rubbed at his face and grinned at me. "What are you doing here?" His question brought me back to my Kitten senses.

"I need to talk to you."

"Sit with me," he said, moving over and holding open his plaid comforter for me. He was wearing the boxers I'd given him for Christmas, the ones with little reindeers on them. He'd been thinking of me! That was awfully sweet of him.

I walked over and sat down, almost ready to forget everything, but then Kira's sobbing voice popped in my head, sniffles and all.

"What's wrong?" Aiden asked. "I don't like to see you frown." He used his finger to trace my downturned mouth. He really didn't like to see me sad. Luckily, I rarely was—it wasn't the Smitten Kitten way.

"It's Darren," I said. "He cheated on Kira."

"What?" Aiden furrowed his brow and glanced around the room, then looked back at me. "Are you fucking serious?"

I glared at him. He rolled his eyes. "Sorry. Are you effing serious?" Aiden raked his fingers through his hair, looking confused.

"I'm seriously serious."

He paused, shaking his head. Then he straightened up. "Wait. Was it with Charlie?"

My stomach flipped. "You knew?"

"No! Of course not. It's just . . . I saw him talking to her after school. I thought it was weird, but it wasn't anything to call him on."

"Maybe you should have."

"Tessa."

"Now you have to, Aiden! Your boys have been out of control lately. Do you realize that every member of the starting five, except you, has cheated on their girlfriend? Do you think that's *okay*?" I felt shaky. I didn't like having to point out something he should have already known. And besides, it was so negative.

"No, I don't. But—"

"Well, then, you need to tell them that. You should be leading them."

Aiden chuckled. He moved over, wrapping me up and putting his chin on my shoulder. "Baby," he said. "They're my friends. And I lead them in basketball, not in life."

"Maybe a life coach is exactly what they need."

"I can't do that."

"I lead the Smitten Kittens! They listen to me. You don't see any of us running around behind our boyfriends' backs." Well, that wasn't entirely true. But at least we weren't cheating.

Oh, butterscotch. I was starting to get choked up. Poor Kira. She'd really liked Darren. They'd been together for close to a month. It was her longest relationship.

"Besides," I said, sniffling. "I should have known."

"Tessa." Aiden pulled back and turned me to him, holding my face in his palms. "There's no way you could have known. It's not your responsibility. You're a Sex Kitten, not the morality police."

I closed my eyes. "It's Smitten." Aiden didn't know about SOS. He had no idea that on the side, the Smitten Kittens were more than the morality police. We were full-on double agents. Like in a James Bond movie—only with twice the sex.

"Lie down with me?" he asked.

I nodded, letting him pull me in between the flannel sheets as disappointment washed over me. I'd let Kira down, and I continued to do something I despised: *lie.*

Aiden deserved to know what I did with the Smitten Kittens; he'd understand. But I couldn't tell him because then he'd know I'd kept something from him for the last two years. I twitched my nose and snuggled closer to him, feeling his heat and trying to block out the negativity.

"I love you, baby," Aiden breathed into my hair as he hugged me.

"I love you too." I closed my eyes.

SOS
CHEATER INCIDENT REPORT

CASE: 043
CLIENT: Caitlyn March
SUBJECT: Michael Garnett
FINDINGS: At approximately 1:00 a.m. on January 30, Mr. Garnett was observed talking online with an unnamed female accomplice. The conversation was not recorded, but judging by Mr. Garnett's actions, we can safely say it was of a sexual nature.

After a thorough phone record search, it was also discovered that Mr. Garnett had been texting obscene messages to a Lisa Belgium. He'd also set up a false MySpace account in order to schedule their meetings. Once retrieved, all the correspondence was sorted. You'll find the transcripts included with this letter.

Note the encounter scheduled on page four. At that meeting, Mr. Garnett and Ms. Belgium were photographed kissing in front of the Seattle's Best coffeehouse. Those photos are included, as well as pictures of Mr. Garnett in front of his computer. Some with boxers, some without.

We trust that this report will remain confidential as some of the information contained within could compromise our top-secret status.

SOS is sorry for your loss, and we offer our deepest sympathies. We hope that we will not have to assist you again in the future, but please keep us in mind for referrals.

Keep smiling,

SOS
Text: 555-0101
Exposing Cheaters for Over Two Years

CHAPTER THREE

"PASS ME THE BOBBY PIN," I SAID, CHEWING ON
the corner of my lip as I fiddled with the padlock on Serena Santos's
metal school locker. I was glad it wasn't a Master Lock—those
suckers took forever to pick! Kira felt around in her blond curls for
a second, then smiled as she pulled out a pin and handed it to me.

"Remembered it this time," she said, beaming. Although
Kira had called me about sixteen more times, her depression over
Darren only lasted until about five this morning. I was proud of her
bravery.

"Hurry, Tess," she whispered, looking both ways down the hall.
"The janitor will be here in twenty minutes."

Sugarplum fairies! I'd better get to it.

I readjusted my stance, checking the half-lit walkway one last
time before I inserted the metal pin into the padlock, twisting and
turning it just right. It clicked.

Kira giggled. "I don't know how you do that. I failed the lock-
pick course three times."

"I remember." Poor Kira. She had a hard time learning new
trades. Now, cheer routines? She was a pro at that.

"I bet Aiden would think it's totally cute you can pick locks."

My stomach turned as I looked over my shoulder at her. "Let's
not think about Aiden."

She grinned, her dimples deepening in her cheeks. "Yeah. Good luck with that."

Kira's blue eyes twinkled as she wiggled her eyebrows at me. I couldn't help it—I laughed. She was right: ignoring Aiden was impossible. And ignoring the guilt I felt for sneaking around was even harder.

"Hey," she said, putting her arm over my shoulders. "Don't look so down, Tess. I'm sure he'd understand if you just told him about SOS."

Kira and the squad knew my inner turmoil about lying to Aiden. And even though they loved Aiden, it was too late for me to tell him the truth. I'd lied for too long. No, I'd just have to stick out the school year. SOS was the Smitten Kittens' secret. I exhaled.

"We have work to do," I said, and yanked open the locker with a metal clang.

Kira reached down to grab the equipment out of the backpack. She pulled out a jewelry-size black box and opened it, revealing the small GPS tracker that Leona had scored a few weeks ago with our frequent shopper's discount.

I took the tiny tracking device from its package and peeled off the self-adhesive back. Then I stuck it in between the pages of Serena's über-thick chemistry book.

SOS had been alerted that she was a "person of interest" in a new cheating incident. Apparently, Paul Masterson had been disappearing between seventh and ninth period every Monday, Wednesday, and Friday. So had Serena. Only, SOS hadn't been able to find where they'd been sneaking off to, and we never accuse without proof. Even if the subjects cheated every time (which they did), we would never tell our clients that. They deserved for it to be definitive. One hundred percent. But it was always 100 percent bad news.

After the chip was settled between the pages, I turned to Kira. "Test it," I said.

She pulled out the SOS phone, punching in the code with a series of beeps. Even though each of us had an encrypted cell, there was only one official SOS line. So at every meeting, we switched possession. It helped to make everyone feel included. Kira especially loved when it was her turn—total self-esteem boost.

There was a blip.

"Easy squeezy," she said, holding up the phone to me. I watched the little red light flash, pinpointing our exact location.

I nodded. "All set." I shut the locker, resetting the padlock, and grabbed up the pack from the linoleum floor. "What time is it?" I asked.

"Almost six."

I groaned. "We'd better jet. Aiden will be at my house for breakfast at six thirty."

There was a sound from behind us, and we froze. The janitor was never early! I put my finger to my lips, signaling for Kira to be quiet, and then we backed against the cold lockers, looking down the hall.

There were footsteps, along with the squeaky wheeling of a mop bucket. Double dang it!

"Shit," Kira whispered. I gave her a dirty look and put my finger sternly in front of my lips again, shushing her.

The squeaking stopped. There was someone right around the corner, just yards away. My heart raced. If we were caught breaking into school, that would be a major violation. I didn't have time for suspension. The playoffs were getting close. Oh, snapdragon! Please just let them leave.

Kira's hand slid into mine. It was sort of sweaty.

Then there was a skidding sound, along with a sloshing, as the footsteps and squeaks went off in the direction they'd come from.

We waited until there was only the sound of the ticking furnaces and buzzing fluorescent bulbs before exchanging a glance. It was getting harder and harder to keep up this covert baloney. I missed just being a regular cheerleader. I missed worrying about high kicks instead of high jinks.

But I was a Smitten Kitten. I had responsibilities.

"Come on," I said, dropping Kira's hand. "I don't want Aiden to get suspicious." I jogged ahead toward the back double doors.

"Now *that* is a good-looking boy," Kira whispered next to me in history class. "Heard he just transferred in from West Washington."

I followed her devious stare over my shoulder to the boy in the back near the bookcase. He was new. Huh—that was odd. Principal Pelli hadn't made me aware of any transferring students, and as head of the Washington High welcoming committee, I should have been informed. I twitched my nose.

"Yeah, I guess," I said, turning back around. Mr. Powell was still at his podium in an animated discussion about the former Soviet Union. It was making my head hurt. He'd obviously had some pent-up anger about the Cold War, whenever that was.

"You *guess*?" Kira kicked at my sneaker under the table. "Look at that hair! He looks like that surfer I dated last summer. Remember him?"

Of course I remembered him. I had seen his sandy rear when I walked in on them at Leona's parents' beach house.

I exhaled and turned again. Sure, he did have that chin-length, chocolaty-cute hair that perfectly framed his strong jaw line. And okay, there were his eyelashes: long and curled, accentuating the soft olive tone of his smooth skin. But—

Suddenly he looked up, staring directly at me. My mouth fell open for a second in surprise, but I snapped it shut and offered a polite smile. He grinned. Slowly, and slightly mortified, I turned in my seat and dropped my head.

"Thanks, K. Now he thinks I was checking him out."

"Well, I *was* checking him out," she said, and then licked her lips. "He's drop-dead delicious."

"He's okay." My eyes flicked up to Mr. Powell. The marker was screeching on the whiteboard as he wrote the names of people I didn't recognize. Wait, Reagan! Ha. One I knew! She was totally from *King Lear*!

Kira giggled next to me. "Sure, Tess. He's only okay." She grabbed her purple pom-pom pen and jotted down something from the board. "You are whipped cream," she mumbled.

When class mercifully ended, I pushed back in my chair and dropped the ridiculously oversized book into my backpack. As I looked down at the speckled linoleum floor, I noticed a Birkenstocked pair of sandals pause and turn to me.

I glanced up the length of the body until I was staring into the face of the new guy, standing there in corduroys and a long-sleeve tee, grinning at me.

Straightening my posture, I pulled my eyebrows together.

"Hi," I said. Wow, he was even better looking up close.

"You're Tessa Crimson, right?" His voice was soft. I relaxed slightly.

"Um, yeah." I slipped into polite mode. I was cheer director for a reason. "Tessa Crimson. Hi."

"I'm Christian. Christian Ferril." He outstretched his hand.

I took it without thinking, but when his cool palm touched mine, I felt my heart rate speed up. He was squeezing me just a little too tightly.

"Nice to meet you," I said as calmly as possible. Where in the world had Kira disappeared? Discreetly, I tried to jet my eyes around the emptying classroom for her. She was gone. Great—it was her fault that I'd looked at him.

"How did you—"

"Know your name?" he finished for me, laughing softly.

I wasn't sure why, but this hot surfer made me uneasy. Like he was in on a joke that I hadn't heard the punch line for yet. I slipped into SOS mode, trying to seek out his ulterior motive, but then stopped. I had to remind myself that I was in school and not on a mission.

"Mr. Powell," he said, tilting his head toward the front of the class. "He told me to see you for the notes from last week. He's making me take the test tomorrow." Christian rolled his eyes. "So he said to ask Tessa Crimson for the materials. And . . ." He shoved his hands in the pockets of his corduroys. "Here I am. Sort of embarrassing myself by rambling."

Aw, it was nice of Mr. Powell to recommend me. Even though I was an A student, I was far from a brain. I'd certainly have to send him a polite thank-you note. I looked appreciatively to his podium.

"Tessa?" Christian asked.

I quickly turned back to him, realizing that I hadn't answered. I shook my ponytail to clear my head. "My notes, right?"

He nodded and his grin widened, revealing a perfect set of teeth. "If you wouldn't mind."

"No, of course not. They're in my locker and I'm going there now, but—"

"Great. I'll follow you." He stepped back, motioning his hands for me to go.

Tentatively, I stood. Aiden would be waiting at my locker for me. How would he feel if I had a new pup at my heels when I met him? This felt odd. And I did not like odd.

Ducking my head, I walked forward into the near-empty corridor. This part of the building only had a few classrooms, so it was quiet, other than the squeaks that my sneakers were making on the shiny linoleum tiles. I suddenly felt a little self-conscious, wishing I wasn't wearing my shorter cheerleading skirt. But Aiden had wrinkled my good one. I smiled to myself, remembering.

"So," Christian said from behind me. "Cheerleading, huh?"

I straightened my posture and looked politely over my shoulder at him. "Yep."

His tone was not lost on me. Being a cheerleader meant getting used to airhead jokes and other stereotypes. That was why I felt it was so important for the Smitten Kittens to keep their dignity intact at all times. Stupid skirt.

"I'll have to admit I'm surprised to get study notes from a person that spends time on the top of a human pyramid. I expected more of the chess club type—"

"I play chess." I swirled to face him. I was pretty sure my bloomers flashed because his grin became a full-on smile. Was he trying to ruffle my pom-poms?

"Really?" he asked, tilting his head and looking me over carefully.

"Yeah." My cheeks felt warm. I didn't like defending my intelligence. Turning slowly, I began to walk forward again. My eyebrows pulled together as I contemplated. Something was off about this boy. Something unusual.

We turned down the busy main hallway, and I immediately spotted Aiden, his head poking out above the rest of the student population. He was resting his forehead against my locker, looking bored. I smiled. Seeing him always made me smile. Forgetting my uncomfortable shadow, I jogged through the crowd and wrapped my arms around my boyfriend's long body from behind. He jumped but then laughed before turning in my arms.

"Hi, baby," he whispered, needing to duck way down to kiss me.

"You smell nice," I said, getting up on my tiptoes to peck him again. He'd just gotten out of phys ed. The boy wore sweat better than any cologne.

"Mm . . ." His hand lightly patted my rear. "You know I love this skirt?"

"I do. I wanted to wear—"

Someone cleared their throat behind me. Right. Notes.

Aiden's smile faltered as he straightened up. Feeling awkward, I pursed my lips and then dropped my arms from around him.

"Aiden. This is Christian," I said, pointing to him. "Mr. Powell sent him to me to get history notes."

My boyfriend immediately reached out his hand to Christian. "I'm Aiden Wilder. I haven't seen you before. Are you new?"

Christian's smile looked forced as he shook hands. "Yeah. We just moved, and I transferred in today from West Washington."

"Ah, a Duck," Aiden said, moving to put his arm around me. "Well, welcome to Wildcats' territory." Aiden was being so polite! He'd sure come a long way with his manners. Not that I minded that he was a little rough around the edges—it was pretty steamy.

"Thanks," Christian said, looking between Aiden and me. "So, the head cheerleader and, I assume, the basketball captain?"

There was that tone again.

"Uh-huh," Aiden said, happily and without a hint of distaste.

"That's cute," Christian replied. I could tell that "cute" wasn't a normal word for him to use. He seemed to choke on it.

"It is." I narrowed my eyes. Odd.

Turning back to Aiden, I put my hand at his hip and tried to move him aside so that I could get to my locker. He did move but leaned down to my ear.

"I've got to take off. I'll see you at lunch." He kissed softly at my lobe and I giggled. I adored his adorableness. "Nice to meet you, Chris," he called as he backed away.

"You too, but it's Christian."

"Right," Aiden said, snapping his fingers. He winked at me and headed off to English class.

Sigh. School would be so much more fun without the confines of the academic system. I glanced back at Christian once as I swirled the combo of my locker without needing to look at it. He smiled.

I quickly turned around and yanked open the metal, pausing for a moment to glance in the magnetic mirror on the door. Hm. I liked this new lip gloss. It had just a hint of pink. Just enough.

Christian chuckled, and I caught his brown eyes watching me in the mirror, seemingly amused. I straightened up and grabbed my stack of notebooks from the top shelf. Flipping through the assorted colors, I found the purple one. I smiled. Color coordination made everything so easy.

"Here you go," I said, holding it out.

"Thank you."

As he took the bound paper, his finger touched mine. He did it on purpose. I could tell by the all-too-innocent expression on his face and the slight reddening of his cheeks.

The bell rang, and I looked up toward the dinging box over the adjacent doorway. Great. As if economics class wasn't bad enough, now Mrs. Foster would make me sit in the tardy chair at the front—the one attached to her desk. Fantastic.

"Try and get it back to me tomorrow," I said to Christian, feeling distressed and tossing a look at him as I slammed my locker door shut with a loud bang.

"Sure thing." With another polite smile, I turned away and jogged toward the end of the hall. I heard a small sound from back by my locker and knew that my skirt was probably flopping up again, showing off my school-colored panties. But whatever, at least they matched.

SOS
INTER-SOS MEMO

FROM: Leona
TO: SOS

As the secretary and treasurer, I have some updates and reminders.

First, the self-defense training class has been changed to Thursday night. Master Marco has asked that we wear our uniforms, but I'm not entirely sure why. Either he's a perv, or he wants us to be prepared in all situations. It begins at seven sharp at the martial arts studio. Make sure to wear bloomers (Kira).

Next up, we just received a large donation in our PO box from Karen McKlusky, mother of Helena. Helena was the unfortunate client involved in that threesome. So gross. Anyway, the money is enough to buy the grappling hook that we were interested in or update our digital recording equipment. We can have a vote after practice on Wednesday.

Also, it has come to my attention that Peter Corning has been soliciting freshmen for dates. Even though he's not technically cheating anymore, he still loses points for being a creep. Keep your eyes peeled for possible violations.

Finally, since Kara Martin is graduating, we'll need to induct a new member into the squad and into SOS. If you know a girl with Kitten potential, submit it to me via text, and I can compile a list for us to look over. As Tessa has said, it's important for the Smitten

Kittens to all be on board with SOS to ensure our top-secret status.
Please have your nominations in by next Tuesday.

That's all for now. Let me know if you need any clarification or
see Tessa with any questions.

Keep smiling,

Leona

SOS
Text: 555-0101
Exposing Cheaters for Over Two Years

SOS
EQUIPMENT ORDER FORM

FROM: Leona
TO: SOS

Our monthly order is ready for Tessa's approval. If there is any last-minute item you need, please write it in and submit it to me before Wednesday.

The order needs to be placed with spytime.com by Friday or we won't earn the frequent buyer discount. The donations this month have been sparse, so please only ask for necessary items. No lip gloss!

ITEMS:
- Portable lie detector—$59.99
- High-resolution tactical camera with night vision—$299.99
- Pen audio recorder—$89.99
- Smart card file retriever—$59.00
- Tubular lock pick—$24.99
- Encrypted Cell–I lost mine!
- Grappling hook
- GPS w/cell assist
- ~~Cherry red lip gloss~~

Keep smiling,

Leona
SOS
Text: 555-0101
Exposing Cheaters for Over Two Years

CHAPTER FOUR

I WAS NEVER SO GRATEFUL TO SEE CORN DOGS.
The loud murmurs in the cafeteria, coupled with the smell of processed meat, were doing a number on me. Economics was miserable. Calculus was worse. All I wanted to do was lay my head on the sticky table and rest my brain. These teachers were seriously impeding my thought process.

"Where were you?" Kira asked, looking at me from across the table with concern. "I thought you'd been Kitten-napped or something."

"My day was totally blown," I complained. "I got the tardy chair in economics."

"Tragic!" Leona said from the other end. "That woman should be stopped. I think Mrs. Foster is inflicting serious emotional damage on the student population with her attendance policies. I'm going to write a strongly worded letter to the school board." She adjusted her glasses.

That was Leona. She was a great asset to SOS. Smart, prompt, and sassy! Sure, sometimes she was a little judgmental (like the time she called Coach Taylor a dictator for making her take a fitness test), but she was a whiz at both computers and fashion accessories. In fact, if I hadn't been so melancholy, I would have certainly found out where she'd gotten her headband. It was fab.

"I like the letters you write," Izzie announced, biting into her corn dog and nodding at Leona. "You have totally great verbiage." Leona thanked her.

Just then, a hand slid across my shoulders, and I looked up, startled. Aiden dropped down in the seat next to me, a bewildered expression on his face.

"You look surprised to see me," he said, taking his arm from around me. "Were you expecting someone else?" He grinned.

"Nope. I'm just depressed." And I was. It was like uneasiness had settled over my uniformed chest. I glanced around the filled cafeteria and wondered how many of the guys in here had been unfaithful in the last two years. Unfortunately, I knew the answer. And it wasn't good.

Aiden's mouth dropped open. "That's not like you. You're like a little ball of sunshine. Always. And I mean *always*. What could you be sad about?" Aiden leaned over to kiss my shoulder, making my stomach flutter. "I'm here, aren't I?"

Indeed, he was here. I had no reason to be sad. After all, I wasn't the one being cheated on. But Darren had been the third adulterer this week, and his indiscretion had totally messed with our lunchtime seating arrangements. I glanced at the empty seat between Kira and Izzie and sighed.

Darren might not have been the first cheater, but he was the first one that we hadn't discovered *on our own*—and that worried me. Because up until now, SOS had been foolproof.

Why were all of these boys going horny? And why did I feel worried when my relationship was healthy?

"We're okay, aren't we?" Aiden murmured into the sleeve of my shirt.

My eyes snapped to his. He *never* asked questions like that! Aiden was pure confidence.

"What? Why wouldn't we be?" I asked, searching his face when he pulled back. His skin was smooth and tan as he widened his green eyes at me.

"Nothing," he said quickly, shaking his head and wrapping both arms around my waist to pull me into him. "I'm sorry, I didn't mean anything by that."

"Hey, Tess," Leona called from the end of the table. "I meant to ask you about the new lollipop in your history class. I heard he is oh, so lickable."

"Ladies," Aiden said, letting me go and pushing away his lunch tray, looking nauseous. "Please don't talk about the men of the school like lollipops. Especially to my girlfriend."

Leona giggled and winked at me from behind her glasses. "By the way," she said as she stood up from the table. "The new boy has a sister, and she's in my algebra class. A real bitch, if you ask me."

"Language," I tsked.

"Sorry. But she is." Leona shrugged, backing up toward the lunch line. "She told Ms. Kellan that she didn't 'do' word problems. Total pout face. And *no* accessories!"

I adored Leona, but maybe she didn't understand that being the new kids at school was probably difficult for Christian and his sister, especially if they'd just moved. I mean, sure, using the word *do* on purpose was sort of tactless, but—

"Psst," Kira interrupted, touching at the corners of her mouth with a paper napkin. "Hottie alert." She darted an excited glance over my shoulder. I was glad she was working on her observation skills. They'd come in handy on missions.

Aiden cleared his throat and grabbed his tray back from

the middle of the table to pick at the salad. He probably wasn't interested in hearing about hot guys. Although I knew that no one was cuter than my sweetie. With that blond hair and those lean muscles, he—

"Tessa?" a soft voice asked.

There was a twinge of irritation, but I recovered quickly and spun around. Christian. Of course. Only this time, he had company: a small, attractive girl with long, straight blond hair and full lips. Her face, however, was pulled into a scowl. At least it was until she noticed my boyfriend. Then her pretty face perked up. Hm. She was checking him out.

"Hello again, Christian," I said, bringing my gaze back to him. I felt Aiden turn around in his seat. I looked sideways at him and he was relaxed, lounging against the table and picking at his fingernails.

Christian took another step closer and smiled at me. "I was wondering if we could join you?" His dark eyes were framed perfectly by his lashes, making his stare intense yet . . . vulnerable.

My heart sank. He was probably embarrassed that he had to ask to sit with us. I couldn't stand to see someone looking so lonely. "Sure," I said politely. "You can sit with us."

Kira let out an excited squeak as Aiden shifted next to me and turned back to the table, still picking at his nails. I watched as the blond girl stared at my boyfriend's dropped head and made her way around to the seat across from him, between Kira and Izzie. She didn't have the same laid-back clothing style as her brother. No, she was more provocative. Or as Leona liked to call it, "slutty"—too-short skirt, low-cut tank top. I swallowed hard. When she finally met my gaze, she smiled—close-mouthed.

"Oh," Christian said, sitting down on the other side of me. "This is my sister, Chloe." He motioned toward her, and she rolled her big brown eyes, as if she didn't like the formal introduction.

Never one to forget my manners, I immediately stretched my hand over the table to her. Just because Leona had a harsh opinion of her didn't mean . . . wait. Chloe looked at me for a second, almost as if the thought of taking my hand repulsed her. The hairs on the back of my neck stood up.

But then she reached out and took my palm in her cool one. She might have thought I hadn't noticed her side glance at Aiden. But I had.

I turned to him, and he was still messing with his fingers, not paying attention. What was with him and his nails? I knocked my knee into his, and he looked up at me, surprised.

"What?"

"Nails," I reminded him. The kid bit his nails to a ridiculous length and then chewed on his cuticles. It was sort of disgusting. I'd tried to give him a manicure, but, well, we never got very far. He always ended up offering to do me instead.

"Sorry, baby," he said, dropping his hands into his lap. "Maybe you can buff them out for me later." He looked sideways at me.

I crossed my legs to control the tingling between them. His stare was devious.

"We'll see." I couldn't help but smile. I loved the snot out of him.

"It's so fun meeting new people," Izzie said happily to Christian as she chewed on the stick of her corn dog. "I think it's really cultural and stuff."

She was sweet. The only redhead in the school that wore the uniform. It was good to have diversity.

Kira cleared her throat and smiled until her dimples were deeply set in her cheeks. "I'm Kira." She reached over the table to Christian, holding out her hand as if she expected him to kiss it.

He chuckled and instead turned it and shook it. Kira's brilliant expression faded briefly, but then she turned to Chloe and smiled again.

"So you're a sophomore?" Kira asked her enthusiastically. She was really great at staying perky.

"Yep. And you're a cheerleader?" There was that tone again. The same one Christian had this morning. Had they been attacked by a roaming band of cheerleaders when they were younger? What was with the hostility?

"I am," Kira said, not at all concerned. "I'm co-captain." She straightened her back with pride. She'd been excited to get that title. Leona had threatened to quit, but we'd resolved it. Smitten Kittens didn't hold animosity toward each other.

"Huh," Chloe said, then looked over at me. "You the captain?"

I didn't like her voice. It was low and gravelly, not cute and small like she looked. It made me think she was not at all the way she presented herself. A wolf in sheep's clothing, if you will. Leona's theory might have been spot-on.

"I am."

"And I'm the captain of the basketball team," Aiden spoke up. I turned to him. He was smiling at her. She smiled back. My stomach felt slightly ill.

Chloe's stare came back to me. I felt pale and not at all cute. She started talking again. "Well, I was surprised when Christian said he wanted to eat lunch with a *cheerleader*, but I guess I can see why. You're prettier than the ones at our old school."

I heard Christian shift next to me. I didn't think his sister was supposed to disclose their private conversation out loud. My pastiness began to grow pink, and my boyfriend didn't make a sound. Biting at the inside of my cheek, I held Chloe's stare.

She brushed her hair behind her ears, looking bored. "Besides, he usually hangs out with smart chicks—like class presidents."

"Chloe!" Christian said through clenched teeth.

"Well, Tessa is the junior class president," Kira announced proudly and pointed at me.

"Really?" Chloe widened her dark eyes, looking sincerely impressed.

My stomach became further ill, and I didn't know why. I had made sure to eat a balanced breakfast! Still, Chloe was bothering me. I wanted her to go away, but I would never say that. It would be rude.

"My Tessa is smart at everything," Aiden said, his voice dripping with admiration. I felt my fist unclench.

"Wow." Chloe held up her hands in apology. "That's really cool. I guess Christian hasn't gone as bat shit as I thought."

"Don't you have somewhere to be?" her brother asked her. I looked next to me to see that his nostrils were flaring as he clenched his jaw.

"No, Christian. I don't."

They stared each other down, neither flinching away. No one seemed to notice but me. The rest of the squad came over to our table, and when Leona returned, she gave Aiden her corn dog. She would never, and I repeat *never*, eat anything served on a stick. My boyfriend looked ecstatic and munched on it like he was a five-year-old at a county fair.

When Aiden leaned over to whisper in my ear, I had already begun contemplating if I wanted to spend time with the school nurse. I was not fond of the way her floral perfume smelled. I'd rather just sign out and leave, but I wanted a second opinion about my gut. It was highly unusual for me to feel this unwell.

"You okay?" my boyfriend asked, kissing my cheek. I didn't look at him.

"I don't feel very good right now."

His hand immediately went to the small of my back. He brought his fingers to my chin and turned me toward him, looking me over with concern. His green eyes were so sweet. I didn't know what was going on with me.

"Let's blow off the rest of the day. I'll take you home." He smiled softly.

It wasn't a terrible idea. I only had one more class and then back-to-back study halls. Aiden was fairly caught up in chemistry. I blinked a few times, and his face darkened more.

"Come on," he whispered, pulling me up.

My head was beginning to ache. I felt dizzy, so I held on to Aiden's arm as I looked at my table. The maroon and gray colors of all the cheer uniforms blended together in a school spirit haze. I got a better grip on Aiden and steadied myself.

"We're going to take off," he said to them. "Tess isn't feeling well."

"You okay?" Christian asked, clearly disappointed at my abrupt departure.

I just nodded.

"It was nice meeting you," Chloe said loudly to Aiden.

"Uh, yeah . . . you too." I could tell by his pause that he forgot her name. It made me feel a little better.

After a second, Chloe looked at me and lifted her hand in a sarcastic wave. "Feel better, prez."

"Wench," Leona fake-coughed.

If I weren't about to throw up, I might have scolded Leona for her language, but at the moment, I was just happy she noticed. Smitten Kitten code was one thing, but out-and-out rudeness by the new girl was another. Christian saw my unease. He mouthed the words "I'm sorry" before Aiden pulled me away.

I lowered my glance and felt a strong arm wrap around me as I hugged him. He moved his cold palm to feel my forehead, then widened his eyes.

"God, Tess. You're burning up."

I stared at him, feeling faint. Something was wrong around here. My Kitten senses were meowing. And I needed to figure out why.

I had a hundred-and-two-degree fever. Really? I hadn't had a fever in years. This would be silly if it weren't so uncomfortable. I shifted on my living room couch, digging my toes into the chenille cushions.

"Are you going to throw up again?" Aiden asked, moving over. His upper lip was curled in disgust, although I knew he was trying to look supportive.

"No. I think I'm done."

"Thank God," he said under his breath.

"Don't tease me. I'm sick."

"I'm sorry. You want me to rub your feet?" There was a devilish gleam in his eye as he looked over my body.

"Stop!" But I laughed. Luckily, the wood-beamed ceiling had stopped spinning after I'd thrown up. Small favors.

"What?" He leaned over and picked up my feet, setting them in his lap.

"Aiden," I whined, leaning my head back into the couch arm. "I can't fool around. I'm sick."

He rubbed at my heel, pressing firmly in just the right places. "It's just that your skin is burning hot. It's kind of turning me on."

I giggled but then winced. My head was effing killing me.

"I'm sorry," he said, leaning over to give my toes a quick kiss before moving them off of him. He stood up and stretched his arms above his head, giving me a peek at his stomach. I sighed.

Aiden smiled and then came over to feel my head. "My poor baby," he murmured, bending down to kiss it tenderly. "Do you want anything before I go to practice?"

I wanted a healthy body, but I was pretty sure Aiden would only offer his own. "No, thanks," I answered with my eyes closed.

He ran his finger gently over my cheek before grabbing his car keys off the coffee table. I listened as he walked through the kitchen to the front door.

After the screen door slammed closed, I lay there with only the hum of the refrigerator to keep me company. Regretting not asking for an aspirin, I let my headache pulsate until I drifted off.

"Tess?"

My eyes fluttered. My mother was standing above me, her graying brown hair frizzy around her face. Her lips were pursed as she pressed her cool hand to my forehead.

"Honey, you have a fever." The wrinkles around her brown eyes deepened as she furrowed her brow.

"I'm sick. Where were you?"

"I just got back from setting up at the club for tonight. Daddy dropped me off, so he still has the car, but I can drive yours if you want to go to urgent care."

"No, Mom. I think I just want to go to bed."

Her face was filled with concern. It was rare that I was this dull. She pulled me up and held my arm as she led me through the house to my bedroom. I lay down on my bed, uniform and all, and snuggled into my white comforter. Once I was comfortable, my mother came back with a glass of water and some Tylenol. Soon, I drifted off again.

Several times my cell phone rang, but I never moved. My mother checked in one last time before she left for the show, but my fever hadn't broken. After I gave her a halfhearted wave, she finally left me alone to suffer in peace.

I tossed and turned all night, dreaming of Aiden and then dreaming of Chloe and her short skirts. I even had an uncomfortably intimate nightmare about being locked in the computer lab with Christian. My forehead was covered in sweat when I woke up.

My body tingled. I looked around my darkened room, trying to get my bearings. It took me a minute to recognize my rosewood dresser, the half-open closet door, and my hanging pom-pom collection. The clock on my nightstand read that it was nearly midnight. Too late to call Aiden.

Even though I tried to relax, I couldn't help but wonder what it was about Christian's sister that made me so uneasy. She certainly wasn't the first girl to eye Aiden. I mean, the boy attracted attention everywhere we went. No. What was bugging me was the way she'd dismissed me. Like I didn't matter. Like I didn't matter to Aiden.

Dang it. I looked back at my phone. I picked it up and scrolled through the missed calls. Kira, Leona, Izzie, my mom—nothing from Aiden. I twitched my nose.

I dialed his number, and as Aiden's house line rang, I chewed on my lip. Please don't let his mother answer. She wouldn't—

"Hello?"

Jiminy Crickets! His mother. "Um, hi. Is Aiden there?"

"Tessa?" She sounded irritated.

"How are you?" I tried to be as sweet as possible, but I knew it didn't matter. She hadn't liked me since that first day Aiden brought me home in uniform.

She tsked. "It's late. He's sleeping."

"I'm sorry. I was sick and I missed his call. . . ." I stopped. She didn't care. "Never mind. I'm sorry I called so late."

"Good night, Tessa," she said abruptly and hung up.

My chest ached as I set the phone back on my table. I didn't like not being liked. Especially when I knew it was so undeserved. I loved her son. I loved Aiden more than anything—

The phone rang. I smiled as I reached out to pick it up. "Hi, sweetie," I said, lying back and cradling the phone to my face.

"Tessa?"

My stomach flipped, and I bolted upright, darting my gaze around my room. It wasn't Aiden. But it was a guy. "Um, yeah. Who is this?"

"I didn't mean to call so late."

"I'm sorry, who is this?" I looked again at the clock; it was midnight! None of my friends would ever dream of calling me this late. A Kitten needed her beauty sleep.

"It's Christian . . ."

Oh, my.

". . . from history class."

I swallowed hard. Cinnamon Toast Crunch! Why was he calling me? First he was in my dreams and now he was on my phone? "How did you get my number?" That might have been a little rude. Guilt crept over me.

"I went to the attendance office and told them that I needed to bring you your assignments, so they gave it to me. I hope you're not mad," he said. "I just wanted to make sure you were okay."

He sounded really embarrassed. He should be! New boys weren't allowed to find my number and then use it without asking me first!

"You really didn't need to call," I said, closing my eyes and trying to get my agitation under control. Being irritable was hardly becoming of a Smitten Kitten.

"I also wanted to ask you about your notes," he said.

My pulse began to calm. Sure, it was midnight and that was an odd time to study, but if it was school-related, he could be forgiven.

"What about them?" I asked.

"They were great. Thanks for letting me borrow them."

"You're welcome." Aw. That was really nice of him to say. I appreciated polite people.

"I was thinking I could come by and drop them off to you."

Sticker shock! What was he thinking? "It's . . . *super*-late." I threw my legs over the side of the bed and eased them onto my carpet, confused and wondering if I'd missed something. Why in the world would he think he could come to my house at any time, let alone in the middle of the night? The tension from my neck seemed to crawl up to my face and rest between my eyes.

"Right. You're right, I'm sorry. Stupid idea. I'll just see you at school tomorrow."

I rubbed at my temple, calming down. "I think that's probably better. Besides, I doubt your parents would appreciate you sneaking out this late." Aiden's mother always hated when he did that.

"Yeah, I doubt my father would even notice if I was gone," he mumbled.

"Oh." I wasn't sure what to say to that. It sounded tragic. "Well, maybe your mom . . . ?"

"Nope," Christian said briskly. "Parents divorced. I live with my dad now. That's why we moved."

Suddenly, I felt awful for being so mean. Divorce! That was something I could understand. "I'm so sorry to hear that. If you want to talk about—"

"Not really," he snapped, cutting me off. "I'll let you get some rest. Good night, Tessa. I hope you feel better."

"Thank—"

He hung up. At first I didn't move, but then I crawled back into my bed and set my phone on my side table. I stared at it. That was a very disconcerting conversation. I had half a mind to call him back and ask him about his parents. Maybe tell him about mine and why I understood.

I chewed on my lip and folded my hands under my cheek as I nestled into my pillow. Even though it wasn't my fault that Christian had called me, I still felt guilty for talking to another guy. Maybe it was the SOS in me. The inner sense of right and wrong. Or maybe I was just really, really disappointed that Aiden hadn't called.

There was another sharp pain in my head. I pulled my blankets up to my chin and tried to think things over. Divorce explained a lot . . . like Chloe's scowl, for example.

And I shouldn't really be mad about the notebook thing. Sure, it was presumptuous of him to think he could call, but maybe that was just his lame pickup attempt. I couldn't fault him for that. Not all guys knew how to properly woo a girl anymore.

I closed my eyes. Aiden had been pretty smooth at winning me over. We were at a school assembly my freshman year, and he'd had to give a speech about recycling. Instead, he got up on the stage in front of all of Washington High, set up a flowchart, and listed "The Reasons Tessa Crimson Should Go Out with Me." He had handouts and everything!

Yeah. Aiden was my guy. He was my perfect, whipped cream boyfriend sundae.

SOS
STOP ORDER

CASE: 044
CLIENT: Becky Roth
SUBJECT: Corey Panchilla

Dear Ms. Roth:

Per your request, SOS shall suspend the pending investigation of Corey Panchilla. This is an official withdrawal from the case.

Although we are pleased that you feel Mr. Panchilla "would never do anything like that," we caution you against engaging in any unsafe practices that may compromise your well-being.

It is also our duty to inform you that Mr. Panchilla will not be able to be reinvestigated because of the laws of double jeopardy.

We trust that this report will remain confidential as some of the information contained within could compromise our top-secret status.

SOS wishes you and Mr. Panchilla continued happiness and hopes that our services will not be needed in any of your future relationships. Have a great day.

Keep smiling,
SOS
Text: 555-0101
Exposing Cheaters for Over Two Years

CHAPTER FIVE

"UH . . ." I MOANED FROM MY BED, MY STOMACH twisting in knots.

"Baby," Aiden said, standing at the edge of my bed and resting his hands on the wrought iron frame. "You can't go to school like this."

"I can't miss practice again," I mumbled, putting the pillow over my head to block out the sunlight streaming in my window. "And if I don't go to school, I can't very well show up in the gymnasium at three thirty." I wished Aiden hadn't pulled up my blinds. My well-dusted furniture was highly reflective, and my room was filled with prisms. They were making me dizzy.

My gut took a sharp turn. "Good golly." I sat up, dazed, nauseous. "I'm going to be sick again."

Aiden walked over, holding my elbow out to help me out of bed. "Let's try and make it to the bathroom this time," he said.

I'd made it as far as the hallway twenty minutes ago. My parents were setting up for a big show in Seattle and wouldn't be back until Monday, so Aiden had to take care of my mess. I bet when he showed up for breakfast, he hadn't expected to find me in this condition. In fact, I don't think Aiden had ever seen me sick, let alone cleaned my upchuck.

"I'm sorry," I whispered as I hung over the toilet. I looked back to see Aiden sitting on the edge of the tub, his elbows resting on the knees of his long nylon shorts.

"You're sick, Tess. Nothing to be sorry about."

I felt a little better. Moving across the blue slate floor, I slid against the wall and looked at him. He stared back at me and smiled softly, but something was bothering me.

"Why didn't you call me last night?" I asked. My eyelids felt heavy, and my fingers were trembling, but my gut wasn't twisted anymore. That was a vast improvement.

Aiden furrowed his brow. "Last night?"

I swallowed, feeling my throat burn, and rested my head against the cool wall. "Yeah. I was sick, and I called you, but you didn't call me back."

"I didn't know you called."

Aiden stood and walked over, climbing down onto the floor in front of me. He reached out to rub my thigh. "I'm sorry, baby," he said quietly. "Figured you were sleeping."

I watched his eyes. They looked honest, worried. I had to remind myself that I wasn't in SOS mode. I shouldn't be looking for signs of guilt, like twitching mouths or upturned eyes.

I exhaled and then got to my knees, trying to stand. "Help me get dressed?"

"Tess, I'm not taking you to school. I'm going to call your mom."

"Don't! They're probably sleeping at the hotel."

Aiden took my hand, helping me to my feet. Then he put his arm around my waist and led me back to my room. "Fine, I won't call her, but you have to get in bed. Now."

"No." I turned, putting my hands on his chest as I tried to make my way to my closet.

Aiden chuckled, taking me by the wrists. "Stop being so fucking stubborn, Tessa."

I shot him a look.

He rolled his eyes. "Don't be so effing stubborn."

"Better." And I knew he was right. There was no way I could function in an academic setting at this point. I needed a day in bed. Chicken soup. Possibly a foot rub.

"Will you come over after school?" I asked. Aiden smiled.

"Baby," he whispered, wrapping me up in his arms and burying his head in my hair. "I'm not going without you. I figured I could stay here and take care of you." He kissed my ear softly, making a little growl.

It felt good. Even though I'd been throwing up all morning, Aiden had a way of still making me feel beautiful.

"You need to go to class." But I put my hands under his shirt against his hot skin, hugging him. Snuggling with Aiden sounded like the best medicine ever. But we couldn't. He was barely passing Language Arts as it was. "Just come back at three."

"Of course I'll come back," he murmured, gently nibbling my neck. "And you better not be sick anymore. I have plans for this weekend."

I grinned, squeezing him a little tighter. "Oh, yeah? What about your mom?" I tilted my head up to give him better access to my skin.

"Don't care." He kissed my collarbone.

"She won't let you sleep here."

"That's why she thinks me and Darren are going camping," he said, mocking my tone.

I laughed. "I love camping." I would have kissed him then, but . . . I'd just vomited. Instead, I moved back and looked up into his green eyes. "I love you," I said.

He winked. "I know you do, baby." Aiden patted my rear before he let me go and pulled back my sheets.

I got on the pillow-top mattress, curling up as he covered me. He leaned down and kissed my forehead.

"Take care of that body for me," he said, smiling.

"You can take care of it when you come back."

He straightened up and walked to the door. "Oh, I will," he called over his shoulder. "Don't you worry about that."

I watched as he left, and when I heard his car start, worry was exactly what I tried hard not to do.

Kira called me at lunchtime. SOS had obtained photographic proof of Selena and Paul. The two had been meeting secretly in the cafeteria storage room. In fact, they'd been hooking up in there. Where our food was kept! Now *that* was tacky. And completely unsanitary.

On top of that, we'd suspended Corey Panchilla's investigation even though the stakeout had already been planned. Sometimes our clients got cold feet. I didn't fault them for that, but it did make our job a little harder. Especially when Leona had already bugged his place.

Plus, we'd gotten a new assignment. It was a good thing I'd let Kira keep the Society of Smitten Kittens' phone yesterday. I was in no shape to organize a mission. She promised to meet with the girls after practice and give them the skinny.

Kira was really improving. Last year, she was a pill. Totally boy crazy. Sort of easy. But I let her join the squad because I could see her potential. I was talented that way: seeing the good in people. And after a few months, she was a total Smitten Kitten. Polite. Sweet. Great at herkies.

Now if only I could find her a nice guy. I'd thought it was Darren. He was handsome, talented, and friends with Aiden, who had even helped get them together. But Darren cheated, and I couldn't understand why. Kira was a natural blonde. Who cheated on a natural blonde?

That reminded me—I still didn't get how Aiden hadn't known about Darren's extracurricular activities. I knew everything about *my* squad. In fact, I even knew that Izzie was menstruating this week!

A quick flash of suspicion flooded me, but I pushed it away. Just because Aiden had seen him talking to Charlie Meyers, didn't mean he knew they were messing around. No. Aiden would never keep something like that from me. SOS was making me overly suspicious, and it was seriously warping my senses.

By the time Aiden came over, I was feeling better. Not a 100 percent, but easily 95. He appreciated it. He practically attacked me the minute he walked in. He was so cute when he had to be away from me.

"I'm missing the uniform right about now," he said as he looked me over at the front door.

I laughed, dragging him by the T-shirt into the house. "I'm not going to practice, remember?"

"Yeah," he said, stepping close to hug me tight. "But I like looking at your legs."

"You need to calm down, Wildcat."

He grinned, then stepped back. "I'm sorry, baby. You're right. I'll behave." He straightened up, looking very controlled. And outrageously hot.

"Good," I said. "I like it when you behave."

Aiden bit on his lip, staring into my eyes before reaching out to take me by the hand. "No, you don't, Tess. No, you don't."

My stomach fluttered. He was right.

SOS
DONATION ACKNOWLEDGMENT

Dear Cathy Hazard,

Thank you very much for your donation. SOS is a nonprofit organization, and your donations go directly to assisting others with their relationship needs by giving us the funding for the latest surveillance equipment.

We are especially grateful for your inclusion of photographs of you and your new college boyfriend. It truly warms our hearts to see our clients happy.

Once again, thank you for your generosity, and we wish you all the happiness in the world. Have a great day.

Keep smiling,
SOS
Text: 555-0101
Exposing Cheaters for Over Two Years

CHAPTER SIX

MY POM-POMS RUSTLED ADORABLY OVER MY
ribboned ponytail as the crowd quieted. The gym was packed,
and the smell of perspiration hung thick in the air. The Wildcats
were winning at halftime. I saved a very special basket toss for
moments like this, mostly because up until this season, the team
had rarely won.

"We've got the spirit!" I called, backing up and stepping on
Kira's thigh as I climbed the length of her body. "We've got the
soul!" Izzie pushed my elbow as I moved from one shoulder to the
next, now three cheerleaders high.

"Let's beat the Beavers!" Leona hoisted me up so that my foot
fit in her palm while I held my other sneaker close to my face. The
crowd was in awe. "What is our goal?"

"Playoffs!" the crowd shouted back.

Showtime. I took a deep breath and with a boost from the squad,
I twisted up in the air, shaking my pom-poms before crossing my
arms over my chest and landing in the weave of arms.

Phew. That was a rush. I was a little shaky as they stood me up.
The entire gymnasium was on its feet. Leona had set up the sign
that my parents had made before they left near the scorer's table.
It read, "The Wildcats Are Grrrrrreat!" in maroon and gray puff
paint. They were so dedicated.

My sneakers squeaked as we crossed the wood floor back to the sidelines just as the buzzer sounded. We plopped cross-legged on the floor, and the players trotted in from the locker room. Aiden winked at me as he ran past, and I felt little butterflies. I loved him after a game. All sweaty and panting. My body tingled. I couldn't wait to get out of here.

"Psst."

I sat a little straighter on my rear.

"Hey, Tessa," someone called from behind me. I turned. It was Christian, just a few rows up, wearing a maroon Wildcats T-shirt. His sister was next to him in a black tube top, watching me with a bored expression. I tried to smile politely.

"Hi," I said, not sure what other sort of greeting was appropriate.

"You were great out there," Christian said. "Like . . . amazing. I'm impressed."

Oh, now that was just too sweet. "Why, thank you, Christian. It's awfully kind of you to say so. Wasn't Kira great, too?" His attention was on the wrong Kitten.

"Uh . . . yeah," he said. "Nice."

Uncomfortable with his seemingly reluctant compliment for Kira, I darted a glance to Chloe. She gave me a thumbs-up, but she didn't smile. In fact, I think she was mocking me. I turned around.

They made me uneasy. Very uneasy.

"He said I was nice," Kira quietly squealed from the floor next to me, rustling a pom-pom in her lap.

I nodded, trying to be enthusiastic. "He sure did. You two are so strawberry smoothie."

She shrugged. "Well, I think he might have a little crush on you. . . ." She reached up to twist one of her curls as she looked down at her lap. Then she looked sideways at me and grinned. "But it's not like he has a chance with you when Aiden's around. And that boy sure isn't going anywhere."

"Nope," I said, glancing out over the court to where Aiden was standing on the sidelines, talking to Coach Taylor. "My boyfriend is total Elmer's glue."

"Definitely." She winked and then turned to look where Christian was sitting and waved to him. I didn't see if he responded, but by Kira's little clap and giggle, I assumed he had.

Still, I didn't feel that Christian had been nearly enthusiastic enough about Kira's cheer. I was going to have to use SOS tactics to find out his deal. And then find out how to get Kira shuffled in his deck.

"Honey," my mother yelled from the front door on Sunday night.

Yay! They were home. I left my calculus book open on my bed and jogged out of my room into the brightly lit kitchen, happy my parents were back.

"Hi," I said, kissing her cheek and reaching out to take her carry-on bag off her shoulder. "Where's Daddy?"

"Oh, he's getting the suitcases." She smoothed my hair back toward my ponytail. "You here alone?" She looked past me into the living room as she set her keys on the granite counter.

"Yep."

"No Aiden?" She frowned.

"He left earlier. Some basketball stuff."

"Oh, darn." She snapped her fingers. "We brought him some gifts from Seattle. We saw a basketball game and bought him a T-shirt."

I smiled. My parents were so good to him. "He'll be back for dinner," I said. "I didn't think you guys were coming in until Monday morning." Although Aiden really liked my parents, he'd certainly be disappointed that we couldn't finish what we'd started this morning. Oh, well. We had the rest of our lives to love each other.

"There's my girl," my father called as he walked in the door, dragging two huge suitcases behind him, his glasses wet with sprinkles of rain.

"Daddy!" I trotted over and hugged him.

"I got you presents." He grinned, taking off his eyewear to dry it on his shirt.

"You guys know you don't have to get me something every time you leave. I'm not five anymore." My father pretended to pout as he put his glasses back on. I shook my head at him.

It was hard to remember the times when we weren't like this. When I was in junior high, my parents had split up. In fact, they'd gotten divorced. I swallowed hard just thinking about it. Luckily, they made up and moved back in together. I had the most happily *unmarried* parents in the world.

"Fine," my father said, lifting his chin. "If you don't want it—"

"I didn't say I didn't want it." I laughed and took one of the suitcases from him, wheeling it into the kitchen next to my mother. My father pecked her on the lips as he passed.

"We sold out the club, Tess," my mother said, stepping behind the counter slab to look through the stack of mail. "Sold out the whole place. They booked us again for the end of the month."

"Wow." I sat down at the kitchen table. "Things are really taking off." After twenty years of playing together, my parents had finally begun to see the success they had wanted—no more private lessons to make ends meet.

It was nice to know that things could work out. In all that time, they'd only quit playing once. When they were divorced.

Shifting uncomfortably at the table, I began to pick at the linen tablecloth. Their divorce wasn't something I liked to think about. It was one of the few things I couldn't see the bright side of.

I had been in seventh grade when it happened. Up until then, I'd always thought my parents were happy. But then one day, my dad moved out. It was awful. The house felt so empty without him here—without the sounds of his saxophone.

My mom began crying a lot. She dropped her music students and spent all of her time writing really sad love songs. Some of which have now become their most requested sets.

When I started splitting my time between my house and my dad's downtown apartment, I found that my parents still had something in common. *Me.*

So I tried to make them proud and keep them both positive. I led by example. Aced my tests, joined cheerleading, and most importantly, I was upbeat. Shiny.

It seemed to work. They both got really into my cheerleading, going to all the games and events, and soon, they were sitting in the bleachers together, sharing a box of popcorn.

After a year of being apart, my dad moved back in. And even though they never technically remarried, they were happy. We all were.

My dad came over and pulled out the wooden chair next to me. I dropped my hands into my lap and looked over at him. He took off his glasses to rub at his eyes and then put them back on.

He smiled at me. "Hey, maybe you and Aiden can come with us next time. I know you two like to watch us play. It might be nice to take a weekend trip together."

"That's a great idea," my mother said excitedly from the sink. She walked over to pull a cup out of the white cabinet and filled it with ice from the freezer. "Seattle is so beautiful at night!"

I nodded. "I'm sure Aiden would love to go. He has fun at the shows."

"Great," my mom said, filling her glass with water. "We'll ask him tonight."

It was nice how perfectly Aiden fit in with my family. And yet I still had the nagging suspicion that I was missing something.

It was seven fifteen, the pasta was on the table, and no Aiden. My parents sat patiently, waiting to eat. The rooms smelled like garlic bread, and my father was practically drooling.

"Did you call him?" he asked, smoothing out the napkin on his lap.

"Yep. His mom said he wasn't home." My boyfriend didn't own a cell phone, and usually he didn't need one. I was always with him.

"I'm sure he'll be here soon," my mother reassured me, patting my hand. She looked at my father. "Have some salad." She pushed the yellow ceramic bowl, overflowing with romaine, in his direction.

My father scrunched his nose and took a sip of his iced tea instead.

The house phone rang out, startling me.

I jumped up, bumping the table with my thigh, nearly knocking over my glass. I apologized before dashing to the phone and snatching it off the counter. "Aiden?" I asked, rubbing my leg.

"Sorry, baby." He was breathing heavily. "We just finished some drills and shit."

I tsked.

"Stuff," he corrected.

"What happened? We've been waiting for you." I sounded whiny, but I'd missed him.

"I know. I can't make it, Tess. Some things have come up."

My heart rate sped up. "Things?"

"Yeah. Just basketball stuff. You want me to come by after? I could tuck you in. . . ." His voice got low and sexy, like he was whispering. I could hear the squeaking of sneakers on hardwood in the background. He was still with the team.

"My parents came home," I said offhandedly because I knew they were listening.

"Already? Shit."

"Aiden."

"Sugar."

I smiled. "You go play with your friends," I said. "But pick me up for school?"

"Of course, baby." I heard the phone shift. "I miss you," he breathed. "I had a fun weekend."

My body tingled, and I was glad my parents were behind me because my face was on fire. "Me too."

"Like *a lot* of fun," Aiden said.

"I know."

"I love you, Tess."

"I love you too."

We hung up, and I took a deep breath before turning around. My parents were both staring at me, concerned looks on their faces.

"No Aiden?" my mom asked.

"Nope. Basketball."

"Well, that's all right," my dad said. "He needs to practice. Aiden has a good work ethic."

I nodded, but I was depressed as I plopped down in my kitchen chair. "Can you pass the salad?" I asked in a quiet voice.

My mother watched me but didn't say anything. Instead, she put some greens on my plate as I set my napkin on my lap.

Monday morning, Kira was waiting for me in the hall outside of history. She looked excited. She started hopping the minute I came into view.

"Tessa," she called, waving to me. It was sort of silly. I was only a few lockers away.

"What's going on?" I asked, looking around at our fellow students, all of whom were staring at us. And not because we were shaking our pom-poms either.

She put her hand on my elbow and led me into the class. "It's the new boy. He's been asking everyone about the Smitten Kittens. Like full-on background checking."

My belly did a somersault. I faced her. She was ecstatic at the news, but I didn't think she realized how bad it could be if Christian dug a little too deep.

"Don't get your curls twisted, K. We don't want him knowing *everything*."

She tilted her head like she didn't understand and then widened her big blue eyes. "Oh, right! Well, from what I've heard"—she got close to whisper—"it's more about our dating lives than our spying lives."

"Really?" I twitched my nose. In a way, that made me even more uncomfortable. "What did he want to know?"

"Dating stats, ex-boyfriends, class schedules—all sorts of stuff." She paused and adjusted the charm on her necklace. "Especially about you," she said.

I watched her, not really sure what to say. I knew Kira had a crush on Christian, and I was 100 percent behind their soon-to-be relationship. But I couldn't help if he'd asked about me. Still, I felt guilty.

"Sorry," I said.

Kira looked over at me and shook her head. "No bigs, Tess. He's a total pup. He just needs to be trained. Like Aiden." She smiled, deepening her dimples, then winked before spinning on her heels and walking through the classroom. She plopped down at our table, leaving me still standing in my flip-flops, sort of stunned.

I'd thought Christian understood the situation. I was with Aiden, and I certainly wasn't available. Now, Kira, she was totally available. And willing. Maybe—

Someone cleared their throat behind me. I blinked quickly and turned. Oh, my.

"I brought your notebook," Christian said, glancing at my feet. I followed his eyes. Red nail polish was smeared across my toes. It made me think about my weekend with Aiden.

"And I'm really sorry about calling you. . . ."

"Tess," Kira whispered from our table. I looked over, and she held up the cell and waved it at me.

Gingersnaps! Another assignment. I hadn't even gotten the rundown on the last one. It seemed like they were coming nonstop lately. SOS was a full-time job.

I looked up at Christian. Poor thing, he was still trying to apologize for getting my phone number. I should let him down easy.

"Excuse me, Christian?" I said in my sweetest voice. I'd hate for him to think I was rude. "I'm sorry to interrupt, but I really have to sit down and sort out my things for class."

His eyes widened. "Sure. Sorry." He motioned forward with his hands.

"No worries," I said. "Maybe I'll see you at lunch or something." There was a pang in my belly. Suddenly his sister's scowl popped in my head. I wondered if it was just because she was sour at her parents' divorce and switching schools. Or—I bit the inside of my cheek—maybe it was because she was interested in Aiden. She wouldn't be the first girl. Luckily my guy didn't notice silly things like that. I swallowed hard.

"Lunch would be great," Christian said, beaming and brushing a lock of his hair behind his ear.

Uh-oh. I wasn't really inviting him. I'd better not do any more damage. I twirled and walked to my table, sitting down in my seat. Pulling my bag into my lap, I grabbed out my history book as I looked over Kira's shoulder at the cell phone screen. Wait.

I turned. Christian was at the end of our table, smiling. I raised my eyebrow. He stared back for a minute.

"Right," he said, holding up his finger like he'd forgotten to tell me something. "I . . ." He laughed to himself and shook his head. "Never mind. See you girls later."

I watched him walk away, feeling a little uncomfortable, and then looked sideways at Kira.

She stared down, tapping her fingernails on the table. "My word," she whispered, shaking her head. "Looks like I have a lot of work to do with that one."

I laughed as she turned around in her seat to smile and wave at Christian. Kira was excellent at keeping a positive attitude. Even though Darren had just cheated on her a few days ago, she was already picking herself back up and moving on. It was brave, really. I was impressed with her tenacity.

"So how did the last assignment meeting go?" I asked when she'd settled down.

"Shit! I forgot." She slapped her hand on the table.

"Kira, language!"

"Sorry, Tess. It just slipped out."

It wasn't like I was the purest soul on Earth, but there was something to be said for old-fashioned manners. And cussing like a sailor was unbecoming of a Smitten Kitten. We were supposed to lead by example.

"So no meeting?" I asked. I should've just come to school on Friday. The girls of Washington needed me. SOS needed a strong leader, and lately, I'd been failing.

"I got sort of sidetracked," she said apologetically.

I exhaled. "By what?"

"Um . . ." Her eyes wandered around the room. Mr. Powell got up, walking to the podium, and opened his oversized teacher's book. I plucked the phone out of Kira's hands.

"Never mind," I whispered. "We'll talk about it later." The bell rang, and I quickly scrolled through the SOS message.

> *911! I think my BF, Marcus Billings, is cheating! I can't catch him, and I've been told SOS is the best. If that bastard hooked up w/ someone else, I will be so pissed b/c we had sex for the first time this wknd. Thx, Cassandra*

I cringed. Sometimes TMI was a given. I handed the phone to Kira and let her read.

"Ew," she said, looking at me with her lip curled. "Too much information."

"I know."

Mr. Powell cleared his throat and told us to open our books to page ninety-six. Kira leaned over to whisper to me, "So when do you want to start this assignment?"

"I can't tonight," I said. "I'm going to Aiden's for dinner. His mother is demanding it." My stomach turned. She did this every few months, mostly to scare me away. But it never worked. I had some very sharp claws for a Kitten, and they were firmly planted in her son's backside.

"Sorry for you," Kira said, pretending to gag. She was so sweet.

"But this weekend," I said. "We need to catch up on these assignments. We're falling behind."

"I know, Tess," she groaned. "But there are just so many. I mean, Darren told me that part of the reason he cheated with Charlie was because I was never around."

"Wait," I whispered forcefully as I touched her arm. "When did you talk to Darren?" Oh, Kira.

She bit her lip. "Late Friday night."

"Gross, K. Breakup sex? You're so above that."

"I know." Her shoulders slumped. It hurt my heart to see her sad, so I gave her a quick hug. When I pulled back, I furrowed my brow.

"But why Darren when you're trying for Christian?" I'd hate to think of Kira going back to her old ways. We'd worked so hard to restore her rep!

She shrugged. "It just happened. Darren sent me a text message, so I called him and . . . Gosh, Tess. I feel awful."

"It's okay," I said, squeezing her hand. "If anything ever happened with Aiden, I would totally still go after him too." My stomach turned. I'd never thought of anything happening to me and Aiden before. I straightened my posture and turned on the captain voice. "Just be careful, K. You're more than a piece of tail. Smitten Kitten slogan."

She nodded. I'd really hoped she'd get together with Christian, but now I wasn't sure it was such a good idea. Not when she was obviously still lusting after Darren. Hm. Maybe I should talk to Aiden. Have him see what Darren's intentions were.

The SOS phone vibrated again. My mouth fell open, and Kira met my stare.

"Another one," she whispered, her dimples deepening with worry.

"Don't respond. We're getting seriously dunked on over here."

Kira leaned back and touched her chest, staring at me. "But . . . you've never purposely not responded to a message."

She was right. What was I thinking? "Okay," I whispered. "Check it, then schedule an emergency SOS meeting for tonight. We'll meet up after my dinner." That was if I made it out of Aiden's house alive. "Can you message the other girls and let them know?"

"On it, Tess." She held the phone under the table out of Mr. Powell's view and began texting. Kira loved when I trusted her with top-secret communications. And even though she messed up the last briefing, I still believed in her. One day, I might even let her lead a practice or two. She'd been trying so hard.

After she put the phone back in her purse, she twirled the gum from her mouth around her finger, staring vacantly ahead. It was easy to see why she always got the attention of the boys at Washington High. She was very orally fixated.

I felt a tingle on the back of my ponytailed neck. Blinking quickly, I turned around. Christian sat up straight as my eyes met his. He beamed. I tried to smile politely, then swung to face front. He was making me self-conscious, but I wasn't sure why. I just had the sneaking suspicion that I needed to keep my distance from him.

Oh, applesauce! I'd have to start after our lunch date.

Veggie burgers. Sigh. Although I appreciated our school's attempt to promote the vegetarian society, I would have been more appreciative if it tasted even remotely like a burger. Besides, it was served with Tater Tots. I wasn't sure what food group they fell under.

"So Tessa," Chloe asked from across the table, tucking her bra strap under the fabric of her tank top. "How long have you been a cheerleader?"

I had hoped when Christian joined us, he'd ask his sister to go to another table, and he did. Only she refused. And took the seat directly across from Aiden. I had my eye on her. And I didn't want to answer her question. I didn't start cheering until seventh grade, the month my dad moved out. In fact, I was a late bloomer. Most of the former squad captains had cheered since Pop Warner.

Kira spoke for me. "Tessa was born in the skirt. She's a natural-born leader. Pure Sex Kitten." Chloe choked on her milk.

I straightened up. "It's Smitten—"

"Holy shit." Chloe laughed in her low, gravelly tone. "Did you just say *Sex Kitten?*" I clenched my jaw.

"Yeah," Aiden said, leaning toward her. "It's a pretty funny story. Everyone calls them that because a few years ago, the Ducks came to town to play us and the point guard found the squad irresistible—especially Tessa." He turned to me and winked. "So, since they cheer for the Wildcats, he started calling them the Sex Kittens. The name sort of stuck."

"Ew, it came from my old school?" She laughed and then looked at me. "You know that name is completely offensive, right?"

My jaw was beginning to hurt.

"Yeah," Leona said from the end of the table. "If I was here then, I would have kneed that Duck in the balls."

"Inappropriate," I whispered.

"That's the thing." Aiden laughed and turned back to Chloe. "Tessa said if she didn't let it bother her, it took away the Ducks' power. That was from Oprah. Right, baby?"

I nodded.

"So she took their power. And I don't know if you've ever seen one of our games, but when the Ducks are here, it's pure entertainment. As soon as the girls stand up on the sidelines, their starting five have all sprung hard-ons."

"Aiden," I said, slapping his leg. There was no need to talk like that. Especially in public. Dressed.

"I'm sorry, Tess. I just think it's hilarious when any guy thinks he has a chance with you." He grinned mischievously.

Christian coughed and shifted in the seat next to me.

My face tingled. Was Aiden acting possessive? I'd never heard him say anything like that before.

"Don't be mad," he whispered, looking over at me. "I'll be a good boy." He licked his lips, taunting me. Daring me to be mad at him. Not possible.

"And how long have you lovebirds been together?" Chloe asked, sounding annoyed. My eyes darted to her. I didn't like her tone.

"Two years," Aiden said, leaning over to kiss my arm and look up at me devilishly. I could see his hands slowly inching down his thighs toward me. He was so naughty.

"Stop," I mouthed to him.

He made a face, scrunching his nose. Then he pulled up, kissed my cheek, and went back to his veggie burger.

"That's a long time to date," Chloe said, looking down and picking through her lunch tray. "You must be so sick of each other." She glanced up at my boyfriend. And smiled.

I gasped. Kira dropped her spork. "Chloe?" she asked. "That is *not* a nice thing to say. Are you effing with Tessa?" Finally. The voice of reason. And it belonged to Kira. Go figure.

Chloe looked around innocently, touching dramatically at her throat. "God, no. I'd never fuck with a Sex Kitten. You guys are obviously badass."

Okay. My heart was racing. I didn't fight and I didn't swear, but I would raise my voice if I had to.

"Goodbye, Chloe," Christian said forcefully.

I didn't look at him; I had his sister's brown-eyed glare locked in my own. She was right about one thing. Nobody effed with a Smitten Kitten.

"Whatever," she said, standing up and pushing her tray to the center of the table.

Her attitude needed to be seriously adjusted. In fact, her overall personality needed a makeover.

She narrowed her eyes at me. "See you around, prez."

My lip curled for a split second, but I caught it. I wouldn't have wanted anyone to know she'd gotten to me. I batted my eyelashes at her and smiled. "Have a nice day."

Chloe flinched like she'd been slapped. Take that. She thought she'd break me. Fat chance. I was a tougher cookie than I appeared. It would take a lot more than a crude word to get me to stoop to her level.

"Goodbye, Aiden," she said sweetly to him, reaching out to touch his arm when she walked by him.

My. Blood. Boiled.

I dropped my head, taking a deep breath before looking back up at the table. No one saw my temporary loss of perkiness. But when I shot a sideways glance at my boyfriend, he was rubbing his arm. The spot where he'd been touched. There was a dull ache I couldn't identify. Cap'n Crunch! Was it doubt?

I felt a hand on my back. I swung around.

"I'm really sorry," Christian said quietly, squatting down behind me. "My sister can be a real bitch—"

I rolled my eyes. Come on with these cussers!

"Brat," he said quickly. "She's a real brat sometimes. I'll talk to her. Make her apologize."

"Thank you, Christian," I said cordially, not unaware that his fingers were massaging my vertebrae. I looked nervously at Aiden, but he was staring down at the table, still rubbing his bicep. I swallowed hard and stiffened my back, waiting for Christian to unhand me. He didn't move.

"Let's go," Aiden said to the entire table just as the bell rang. He was up and staring down at Christian and me before the ringing had even stopped. He didn't look jealous. He looked fine. I blinked quickly. Maybe he *should* be a little jealous.

"Nice seeing you again, Chris," Aiden said, grabbing my backpack off the cafeteria floor. I stood, letting Christian's hand fall from my body. My fingers were trembling from the altercation with Chloe. Coupled with Christian's need to touch me, this had been a very odd lunch.

"Yeah, you too," Christian said, eyeing my boyfriend.

I slid my hand into Aiden's as we began to weave through the tables on our way to the hall.

"By the way, it's *Christian*," Christian called from behind us.

"Right. Sorry," Aiden replied, but didn't turn around.

I smiled. Maybe he was jealous. I held his hand a little tighter.

SOS
INTENT TO INVESTIGATE

CASE: 045
CLIENT: Mandy Morgan
SUBJECT: Travis Murray

This is the SOS official notice of intent to investigate Travis Murray. The client has accused Mr. Murray of "stepping out with his ex." It is unclear whether the subject had terminated his previous relationship or "gone back for seconds." The investigation will begin in 48 hours.

If you wish to cancel this investigation, please text a stop work order to 555-0101. Stop orders must be placed within 24 hours of this written notification.

We trust that this notice will remain confidential as some of the information contained within could compromise our top-secret status.

Thank you for thinking of SOS, and we truly hope that our investigation ends with positive results. Have a great day.

Keep smiling,
SOS
Text: 555-0101
Exposing Cheaters for Over Two Years

CHAPTER SEVEN

I SHOULD HAVE ENJOYED GOING TO AIDEN'S HOUSE.
It was really nice. An old Craftsman with intricate woodwork and
oriental rugs, filled to the beams with beautiful furniture from
around the world. It was also, however, filled with his mother's
scorn for me.

"How's cheerleading going?" she asked. Her green eyes,
creased at the corners, were boring into my face.

"Very well. Thank you for asking." I smiled at her and then
looked across the table at Aiden. He was avoiding her, rolling pasta
onto his fork. I wished I could avoid the conversation too.

"That's nice," she said. It sounded forced. She hated me. "And
your grades?" she asked.

"Tessa's on the honor roll again," Aiden said. Aw. I loved it
when he was proud of me. I gazed lovingly at him.

His mother didn't seem as appreciative. "Well," she said,
sucking on her teeth. "Maybe if you two spent less time together,
you'd be on the honor roll too, Aiden."

There was a hiss in my throat, but I forced it down with a sip
of water. Aiden didn't need to be on the honor roll. He was a great
athlete and a total sweetheart. Studying just wasn't his thing. She
didn't adore his adorableness as much as I did.

"Tessa," his mother said sternly from the head of the table.

"Are your parents at all concerned with the amount of time you two spend together? And the late nights?" It was the last part she really didn't like. Her eyes narrowed on mine.

"Uh, not really," I said honestly. "My parents love Aiden, and they trust him."

Mrs. Wilder set down her fork with a clank and took a deep breath. Here it comes.

"Look, Tessa," she said in fake sweetness. "I think you're a really nice girl, I do. But I just don't think it's healthy for two teenagers to be together as much as you and my son are. You guys really need a break from each other."

Even though I knew she'd say it—again—my face stung. I *was* a nice girl (I was glad she'd noticed), but Aiden and I were far from unhealthy. We loved each other. Healthily!

"Mom," Aiden pleaded, tossing his napkin on the table. She glared at him. He got quiet, and I closed my eyes. Sometimes I just wanted him to speak up.

"You really want to go away to college in such a serious relationship? Without ever having dated anyone else?" she asked, looking at him angrily.

I clenched my fists under the table. That was not okay. Aiden didn't need to date anyone else. He didn't even need to *consider* dating anyone else.

"Please, just stop." Aiden dropped his head in his hands as his elbows rested on the table. He hated fighting with his mother.

She exhaled. "I'm sorry," she said, although I knew she wasn't. "It's just . . . I married my high school sweetheart and look how that turned out." Aiden shifted uncomfortably. "I just want something better for you, Aiden. You have a real chance to make a great life for yourself. You're a tremendous athlete. You should be focused on school and basketball. I think Tessa has been a huge distraction for you."

I stood up and folded my napkin neatly, setting it next to my nearly untouched plate. There was only so much I could handle without losing my stuffing. "Aiden," I interrupted. "I'd like to go home. Can you please bring me?" Shoot. I should have driven myself.

Aiden pushed back in his seat with a loud scrape and gave his mother a disappointed expression. She looked down in her lap. She'd lost this argument.

"I'll see you at the game, Tessa," she said, not looking at me.

"Thanks for dinner," I whispered, unable to lift my head. My chest hurt. I wanted her to like me. I really did. Especially since I loved her son so very much. But . . . she didn't. And there was nothing I could do about it. I nodded and walked to the door.

Aiden whispered something to his mother, but I didn't catch it. He wouldn't go home tonight. She knew that. And that was about as rebellious as he got. Tomorrow he'd be back here and they'd get along until the next time we had dinner together. It was a vicious cycle of passive aggressiveness.

Aiden met me at the door, looking down into my face. My cheeks were burning with humiliation and sadness. I sniffled.

His eyes weakened. "Come on, baby," he said, opening the front door for me. He put his hand on my shoulder and led me out.

The night was cold, and I shivered against it. When we paused at his car, Aiden reached out and completely wrapped me up in his arms. He kissed my mouth forcefully, taking my breath away. When he moved back, I was gasping and feeling decidedly better.

"Well, that was nice," I said, trying to smile at him.

"I love you," he said seriously, as if I were arguing that he didn't. "I love you so fucking much." My bottom lip jutted out. Aiden looked like he was going to cry, and I'd never let him cry.

I nodded. "I know you do."

"There's no break. Don't listen to that bullshit. It's not going to happen."

I raised my eyebrow at his language but didn't say anything. When he was like this, he was allowed a bad word or two. His mother was a real *b-i-t-c-h* sometimes.

But my sweetie still looked distressed. I knew it was because his mother had brought up his father. Aiden was really sensitive about that. And who wouldn't be? His dad had left them when Aiden was twelve. He never called, never wrote, nothing. How anyone could forget about Aiden was a crossword puzzle to me.

"Tell me no break," he whispered, kissing me with his eyes open.

I reached up and swept his hair away from his face. "You're not going to shake me, point guard. I play man-to-man defense."

He grinned. He thought it was so cute when I talked basketball. Aiden bent down and kissed my neck softly. "I'm sleeping at your house tonight," he mumbled into my skin.

"I figured as much," I said, biting my lip. My hands slid down to his waist.

"And we're going into overtime tonight, baby."

I laughed. "Let's get out of here," I said, moving back. "Your mom's probably watching out the window." I glanced over, and she totally was. Ew!

We got into Aiden's Jetta, leaving for my house. I pushed his mother's dirty looks from my mind and imagined next year. Aiden away at Washington State and me still cheering with the Smitten

Kittens. We'd be apart, but we'd work it out—we belonged together. We were apple pie à la love.

"She brought up his dad?" Kira asked over the phone, sounding completely sorry for Aiden. I shifted the receiver to my other ear, listening for Aiden, who was taking a shower in the hall bathroom.

"I know," I said to Kira, walking over to my mirror to check my lip gloss. "I felt awful for him. Just because his dad is a complete jerk doesn't mean that all relationships are doomed to fail. That woman seriously needs some sunshine in her life."

"Or maybe Prozac," Kira said. I grinned and stepped over to my bed, dropping down and sinking into the pillows.

"Sorry about canceling the meeting. You sure you guys don't mind waiting until tomorrow?" I hated blowing them off, but Aiden was here. There was no way for me to sneak out with him in my bed.

"No bigs," Kira said. "But we have some pending assignments. Travis Murray is accused of hooking up with his ex-girlfriend, or at least, I think she's his ex. Either way, it's going to be a busy week."

I sighed. "I know. And thanks for listening, K. About Aiden's mom and all. She really messed with my head tonight. I wished Aiden lived here with me; it'd be so much easier."

"Oh, I'm sure you'd take *good* care of him." Kira giggled.

"Be quiet." But I was smiling. She'd done one heck of a great cheer-up job tonight. The shower in the bathroom turned off with a squeak.

"You and Aiden are like Romeo and Juliet," Kira said dreamily. "It's like star-crossed lovers and—"

I furrowed my brow. "K, Romeo and Juliet killed themselves."

She gasped. "Oh, my word! They did? That is so tragic!"

I held back my laugh. "Hey," I whispered. "Aiden's out of the shower. I'll talk to you in school tomorrow."

"Night, Tess. Give Aiden a big, sloppy kiss for me." She giggled.

"Yeah," I said. "Probably not sloppy, though." Because that would be gross.

I hung up and set the phone on my side table just as my bedroom door opened. I sat up, admiring Aiden's lean, wet body draped in just a towel. He noticed.

"Hey," he said, leaning against the door frame, rubbing another towel in his hair. As I watched him, he wiggled his eyebrows and tossed the wet cloth at me.

It bounced off my shoulder, and I laughed. "Hi."

"Who were you talking to?" He licked his lip, readjusting the towel around his waist.

"Kira."

"What's up with her?"

My insides were complete pudding right now. "She wanted me to give you a big, sloppy kiss."

"Sloppy, even? That sounds sort of hot."

I smiled and shook my head. "Quit teasing me and come over here." I patted my bed. I wanted him. I always wanted him, and there was nothing his mother could say to change that. We didn't need a break; she was wrong. In my heart, I knew she was wrong about us.

SOS
CLIENT REJECTION

CLIENT: Becky Roth
SUBJECT: Corey Panchilla

Dear Ms. Roth:

SOS is sorry to inform you that your cheater request has been denied due to the rules of double jeopardy. Although we sympathize with your discovery of a "skanky thong" in the glove compartment of Mr. Panchilla's car, we are unable to investigate further.

It may be in your best interest to confront Mr. Panchilla yourself or possibly terminate the relationship.

We trust that this report will remain confidential as some of the information contained within could compromise our top-secret status.

Please keep in mind that double jeopardy does not apply to your future relationships. SOS is still at your service, and we hope you'll keep us in mind for referrals. Have a great day.

Keep smiling,
SOS
Text: 555-0101
Exposing Cheaters for Over Two Years

CHAPTER EIGHT

"UH, TESS?" KIRA WHINED AS WE PAUSED ON THE multi-color carpet of the restaurant aisle. "Why are we inside? We could scope this out from the car. My hair is totally going to smell like french fries."

"Shh . . . we're supposed to be incognito."

"In *what*? I thought we were undercover."

I rolled my eyes but then reached down to tug up the legs of my black stockings. Irk. These things were annoying. And fashionably hideous. I had to leave my utility vest in the car, but I still had on the black turtleneck and stockings that went underneath it. Right now, I looked like a mime—minus the white gloves.

Marcus dragging his date to the Applebee's two towns over was inconvenient, but he wasn't nearly as smooth as he thought. Not when we'd already bugged his cell phone. My breath caught.

"Snap, crackle, and pop!" I whispered harshly. "They're early." I ducked down, then dropped to my knees, pulling Kira under a booth table with me.

The carpet was rough, and I hadn't expected the space under the booth to be so tight. Kira was practically sitting in my lap.

"Ew," I said, trying to push her back. "Your hair does smell like fries."

An immediate pout pulled at her pink lips.

"Is this table okay?" Leona's sister's voice announced. Her black sneakers paused in front of us. Her undercover work as a waitress was usually pitch perfect. But what was she doing? They couldn't sit here! There was no room for their legs.

"Naw. How 'bout the one toward the back?" Marcus asked in his usual smooth, confident voice.

I exhaled as I watched the feet move away, noticing the pair of red heels that followed Marcus's sneaks. Really. Red? That seemed sort of tacky, even for Applebee's.

"Wow," Kira said, adjusting herself in my lap. "That was close."

"Not as close as us right now," I said, moving her over. I tried to unfold my legs in the darkened area under the table, but it wasn't big enough. Well, this wasn't very fun. And it wasn't easy to stay in spy mode when I knew I could be at the movies or making out in the backseat of a car—something normal. I twitched my nose. "Is Izzie taking care of the video feed in the car?"

Kira nodded, trying to smell her hair. I'd let Izzie drive tonight. It helped her feel more involved. And even though she wasn't great at things like math or science, she was awesome on the feed. Total pro.

"Let's go," I whispered, sliding myself up onto the seat. I opened a menu in front of me and then peeked over it toward the back of the restaurant. Uh-oh. Marcus's face wasn't in view. No clear shot. I'd need to get closer. I bent my head back under the table to Kira.

"K, hand me my camera." She rummaged through the backpack, pulled out the extra-zoom lens, and snapped it on the camera before handing it to me. "You move in," she said, widening her eyes. "And I'll listen to the audio. But be careful."

I nodded. She always worried about me. The thing was, if

the Smitten Kittens were found out to be SOS, the guys in the school would freak. To this day, all the cheaters thought that their girlfriends had caught them. If they knew what the squad and I had been doing for the last two years and some of the things we'd seen, they might not appreciate our cheers anymore. In fact, they might boo us.

I shuddered. That was a very negative thought. Lately, SOS assignments had seemed to be bringing them out in me. Something about the fact that 100 percent of all of our assignments ended up in a cheating confirmation was depressing. One hundred percent of the time.

"I've got the audio feed," Kira whispered, nudging my leg. "Video is recording from the bar, but there's not a clear view. Wait . . ." She touched her earpiece. "Marcus just told the accomplice that he has to . . . drain the lizard."

We looked at each other and giggled. Honestly. How some of these boys scored was beyond me.

"Move in," Kira said, waving her hand.

Keeping my head low, I moved to the booth across from us and peered over the top. Marcus was gone. I needed to get at least two clear shots for the report. Preferably one with them holding hands or kissing. I swallowed hard. I hated this part. Witnessing the cheating. It made me pretty sick, and sometimes, it even gave me nightmares.

Before he could come back, I'd made it to the large plastic fern a few feet from their table. I wasn't used to being this close to the action. I had both audio and visual. Holding up my camera, I clicked off a few silent shots of the girl. I didn't recognize her. She must be from a rival school. Marcus was a traitor.

He came back, kissing her cheek before he sat down. I felt the familiar turn in my stomach. The girl was beaming at him. Did she know he had a girlfriend?

"Where's your girlfriend tonight?" she asked, sipping from her water. My lip curled. She did know. That was bad form, even from a rival school.

"She's studying." Marcus licked his lips suggestively, eyeing her cleavage. He reached out to touch her fingers. "She has no clue."

"That's good," Red Heels said. "I'd hate to kick her ass if she tried to start something with me."

"Naw, she's not smart enough to figure it out. She won't mess with you."

My throat was burning. I wanted to yell out. I wanted to scream. But instead, I took another picture as he reached under the table to rub Red Heels's thigh. My nose began to run. I needed a tissue.

I took out my phone, punching in the escape code to Kira. Within a minute, Leona's sister appeared at the table, talking animatedly and blocking their view of the plant. The restaurant music turned up to a much louder level and I began the move.

The music disguised the rustling of the plant as I slid from behind it. I walked quickly and purposefully toward the door. Not looking back, not looking down. Cool and collected.

As I passed the last table, someone grabbed me by the wrist. I gasped.

"Tessa?"

Christian? Toasted ravioli! I was busted. I was busted being in Applebee's with the cheater. My heart pumped and I jetted my eyes around for Kira. I found her by the front door, her eyes wide and frightened.

"What . . ." Christian paused, covering his mouth with his other hand as he looked me over. "What are you wearing?"

I needed to take control of the situation. Sure, I was dressed in black from head to toe. But this could be normal. If I played it normal, it could be normal.

Shaking my hand from Christian's grip, I looked around at his table. He was with two others, but I didn't recognize them. They were probably Ducks.

First, I needed to dodge the fashion question. "Sorry, Christian. My ride is leaving." I looked back toward Kira, who was now hiding behind the hostess booth, watching nervously.

"You're leaving?" Christian asked, looking disappointed. "Well," he said anyway, motioning to his company. "This is my best friend, Colton, and his girlfriend, Sherrie."

I smiled at them, offering a little wave. I needed to get out of here before anyone else saw me. Someone who knew I'd never dress like this. That was the number-one rule of the Society of Smitten Kittens—never be seen at the location of the incident. Christian had seen me. This was a huge complication.

"This," he said to them, reaching out to touch my hip. I was startled. "This is Tessa Crimson."

I sidestepped his hand, trying not to look as thrown off as I felt. He wasn't allowed to invade my personal space. And my hips were very personal.

"Oh," Sherrie said, pursing her dark red lips. "The cheerleader?"

I blinked rapidly. Whatever school they came from, I'd have to meet their cheer captain and find out about the animosity factor. This was getting ridiculous. She was smirking at me.

"I'm sorry," I said, backing away into the aisle. "I have to go."

Christian tilted his head. "You sure?"

Wow. He was more aggressive than I had originally given him

credit for. Maybe with his friends, he was more confident. Either way, he seriously needed to be avoided. Especially now that he'd seen me on assignment. "Yeah. Bye." I nodded to them and twirled quickly, striding toward the door. I could have sworn I heard a snicker as I left.

Kira jumped out just as I passed the hostess booth, but she waited until we got outside in the cool night to totally freak out. "Oh, my word, oh, my word . . ."

"Breathe," I told her, taking her by the shoulders even though my own voice was tight. Nervous. "Let's get out of here. Quick."

She nodded and we began to jog across the asphalt parking lot toward Izzie's blue Honda. Her face was white as we opened the doors and climbed in.

"Well." Izzie gulped. "What happens now? The new boy saw you. Are we compromised?" She'd obviously seen the video feed.

I put my hands over my face and bent over, trying to think. Okay. So yes, I'd been spotted. But SOS communications always stayed top secret. There was no reason for Cassandra to use our evidence to confront her boyfriend. We could destroy the photos. She could just say she knew. Crab cakes! I'd never give an official ruling without hard evidence.

"Maybe we should just abort," Kira said quietly from the backseat. "Tell Cassandra we didn't find anything."

I swallowed hard and looked up. I just couldn't do that. I couldn't let Marcus get away with it.

"We're fine," I said to the girls, my back straight. "Let's hang out for a bit, and then we'll follow them. I want to wrap this one up."

Kira and Izzie exchanged a glance but then nodded and agreed. I was glad they did. Because I wasn't sure what I'd say if they argued. I had the feeling that Christian Ferril was going to a big, honking problem.

SOS
CHEATER INCIDENT REPORT

CASE: 046

CLIENT: Cassandra Heart

SUBJECT: Marcus Billings

FINDINGS: At approximately 7:00 p.m., February 6, Mr. Billings was observed having dinner with an unfashionable female accomplice at Applebee's restaurant. They were photographed holding hands and using their feet under the table to fondle each other.

The pair was later followed to a parking area overlooking Skinner Butte. Photographs documenting the interaction were unclear due to the fogginess of Mr. Billings's window. SOS did, however, recover an item that Mr. Billings tossed from his driver's window, confirming sexual intercourse.

We trust that this report will remain confidential as some of the information contained within could compromise our top-secret status.

SOS is sorry for your loss, and we offer our deepest sympathies. We hope that we will not have to assist you again in the future, but please keep us in mind for referrals.

Keep smiling,

SOS
Text: 555-0101

Exposing Cheaters for Over Two Years

CHAPTER NINE

CASSANDRA WAS LESS THAN THRILLED TO SEE the glossy eight by tens of Marcus and Red Heels. It nearly broke my heart, especially when I considered her recently departed virginity. All of it left me feeling, well, bummed.

I watched from my locker across the busy school hallway as Cassandra unfolded the manila envelope I'd left there. Her face broke, then she recovered and glanced around quickly. Brave soul; she didn't want anyone to see her cry. My chest ached.

Turning back to swirl the combination of my lock, I tried to decide what sort of flowers to send her. It should either be daffodils or daisies. I always sent flowers after I delivered bad news. It helped with self-esteem.

"Tessa?"

I jumped. When I turned, I was alarmed and certainly dismayed to be looking back into the dark brown eyes of Chloe, Christian's sister. Hm. There was that forced smile again on her red lips. This couldn't be good.

"Yes?" I asked, flipping my hair over my shoulder to cover my nervous twitch. Her smile turned into a smirk. She adjusted her stance in her open-toe heels.

"I just wanted to apologize for the other day at lunch. I know I was being a bitch, and I'm sorry."

I blinked, then nodded. No need to argue with that.

"Anyways," she said, staring down at her shoes. Her toes had only clear polish on them, and somehow, that set me a little at ease. She continued, "I just wanted to say that I was sorry and that I'm looking forward to hanging out with you this weekend."

My stomach dropped. She obviously noticed my surprise because her full lips spread into a real smile. Not the fake one I'd gotten to see earlier.

"This weekend?" I tried to sound casual, but there was definitely an absence of perk in my voice. I looked around the hall, feeling my uneasiness beginning to make me shaky. What was going on?

"Oh," she said, a little *too* surprised. "Aiden didn't tell you? He invited me and Christian to his party this weekend."

Aiden was having a party? I shook my head, trying to remember if he'd told me about it. Maybe he did, but I wasn't sure. SOS had been so busy and . . . Wait. Aiden invited them?

"When did you talk to Aiden?" I asked. Was it normal to see little black spots in the corner of my vision? That had never happened before.

"I'm in his chemistry class," she said. "We're lab partners. You didn't know?"

Oh, sweet vanilla sky! I was going to be sick. I put my palm against the cool metal of my locker to steady myself. Was I still ill from last week?

"Well," Chloe said, licking her teeth as she slowly looked me up and down. "I'll see you at lunch."

I was frozen as I stood, watching as she turned and walked away. Her long blond locks swayed from side to side, brushing against her back and her short pleated skirt. My face was numb. There was a violent turn in my stomach, and I clutched at it. I dashed down the hall, barely making it into the girls' bathroom. After two dry heaves and an unceremonious flush, I straightened, unsure as to why I'd been so sick lately. I was losing my grip. Somehow, Chloe had gotten under my skin. But what was it that made me so unnerved around her?

Stepping out of the stall, I studied my reflection, disappointed to see dark circles under my eyes and my furrowed brow. I twitched my nose and put back my shoulders. I needed to know more about her and her brother. I was the head of the Society of Smitten Kittens. I should know more by now.

The bell rang, and I sighed. I was late for history. This day had certainly not started well. Not well at all.

I debated using the menstruation excuse to get myself out of lunch detention, but in the end, I decided to take the high road. What sort of example would I be if I lied to get out of punishment? Not a very good one. And I had a liar quota. One I had already filled with SOS.

I could see Kira's admiration as I stood listening to Mr. Powell scold me in front of our class. Her steely blue eyes told me that she wished she were as brave. It made me feel a little better.

After I'd gotten to my seat and recovered from the in-class humiliation, Kira slid a note over to me. I gave her a disapproving look but opened the folded notebook paper anyway.

You just missed it, it said. *Christian got lunch detention like five minutes ago!*

My pulse sped up. Fantastic. The person I wanted to avoid would now be alone at my side for the entire forty-three-minute captivity. I couldn't take any more bad news. I needed Aiden.

Only, when I got out of class, Aiden wasn't waiting at my locker.

I stopped, mid-stride, and spun around the crowded hallway. Where was he? After another second, I continued my disconcerted walk to my locker. I twirled my combo with little grace, dropping my notebooks on the linoleum floor as I fumbled with them. Before I could be late again, I scooped them up and slammed my locker shut, trotting off to economics. Alone.

My cell phone was dead from my forgetting to charge it the night before, and I felt cut off from the outside world as I sat miserably in class. I was beginning to perspire. My day had been so awful that I was sweating without actual physical exertion! I was on the verge of tears. It was Leona's turn with the SOS phone, and she had already informed me in between classes that we'd gotten a new assignment last period.

I felt overwhelmed. And since Aiden sat with us at lunch, the Kittens and I wouldn't be able to discuss the assignment there. We'd have to wait until after practice. Not to mention, I was wondering where in the stratosphere Aiden was. I hoped Kira would pass along my tale of lunch imprisonment to him. He had to be looking for me. Right?

I signed the journal on Mr. Powell's desk as I entered detention. I frowned as he smiled at me. I didn't mind letting him see me pout. I'd been in his class last year too.

"Sorry, Ms. Crimson," he said, wagging his finger at me. "Rules are rules. Even for the head cheerleader."

That was sort of nice of him to apologize. I nodded. Feeling dull and wilted, I crossed to my table and flopped in my chair. It figured I'd only finished half of my apples and cinnamon oatmeal this morning. I was starving. There was a shuffle from the hallway.

I looked toward the door as Christian entered, grinning madly as he swiped his hair behind his ear. He avoided my eyes, but I could tell he wasn't too broken up about sitting in detention with me. Not with that pleased expression on his face.

Christian signed in and then turned to me, pretending to be surprised. "Tessa," he said, clutching his chest. "I had no idea you were a troublemaker."

I couldn't help but smile. His theatrics were sort of cute. "Sorry, Christian. But there is no talking in detention." I looked down at my purple notebook. Hm. Maybe I'd write a note to Aiden. I was pretty sure that was how things were done before text messaging. I opened to a fresh page.

"Can . . . I sit with you?" Christian asked.

I glanced up. He was trying to sound casual, but he probably didn't realize he was biting his bottom lip. I wondered if I made him nervous. He certainly made me feel unsettled.

"Just sit down somewhere, Mr. Ferril," Mr. Powell announced from the front, sounding annoyed. I giggled.

Despite this being detention, it actually wasn't very strict, especially in this classroom. Mr. Powell had a tendency to read the newspaper instead of enforcing the law. I liked that about him.

Christian was still standing at the end of the table, so I nodded toward Kira's chair, and he smiled as he sat down. Wow. His cologne smelled rather good, very natural and earthy.

"So," he said, drumming his fingers on the table. "How long do we have to stay in here?"

"Until ten minutes before lunch is over." I looked sideways at him, noticing that his hair had fallen to cover his eyes. I didn't really like that. It seemed sneaky.

"Good," he said, leaning back and turning to me. "Because I'm ravenous. I thought I had to miss the entire lunch."

"I don't think that's legal," I pointed out.

"Right."

We sat for a minute, silent, but not uncomfortably so. Somehow, being alone with him was easier than being near him with an audience. Go figure. Mr. Powell turned the page of his newspaper loudly and hunched over to read.

Christian leaned toward me. "Would you like to know anything about me?" I looked at him, and he smiled that perfect grin. I couldn't really think of anything, but . . . I didn't want to seem unfriendly.

"Sure. Did you like being a Duck?" I adjusted myself in the chair, folding my hands onto my lap.

"Yep. My turn."

Wait. I didn't know this was a give-and-take.

He cleared his throat. "Why are you so proper? Like with the swearing and everything?"

I blinked. It had been a while since I'd needed to explain my perkiness. "It's not that I'm proper, Christian. This is just how I am. I'm perky. I'm polite. There's no need to be all gloom and doom. Someone has to make people feel good."

Christian pressed his lips together, looking impressed, and nodded. "You definitely are *not* gloom and doom."

That was nice of him to say. And truth be told, I wasn't always like this. There was a time when I was just like everyone else. But my parents liked me like this. In fact, everyone did, so it just stuck. It felt natural. I liked making people happy.

"Your turn to ask," he said, folding his hands behind his neck and leaning back in the chair. I glanced at the clock. We still had twenty minutes together.

"When did your parents get divorced?" I asked softly.

His expression changed. He rubbed roughly at his jaw and then straightened his back. "Officially?"

I nodded. I hoped the question wasn't too painful.

"Last month."

"And that's why you're here?"

He looked me over. "Don't feel sorry for me, Tessa. You know, at least half of all marriages end in divorce." He narrowed his heavily lashed brown eyes. "And like 99 percent of high school romances don't last."

My face twitched. Was he trying to say that Aiden and I wouldn't last? "You really don't know me all that well, Christian." And he certainly didn't know that I was fully aware of the breakup statistics. I did it for a living, for Pete's sake.

"True," he said, backing off. He laid his hands on the table in front of him. "And how about you? What's your family like? Do you live in a gingerbread house somewhere?"

"I, in fact, live in a ranch-style home in Murray Hills. No candy roofs or evil witches." Well, except for Aiden's mother.

"And I'm guessing your parents are living happily ever after?"

I dropped my eyes. Even though my parents were happy, it still didn't mean there weren't painful memories. "My parents got back together after some time apart."

Christian made a noise, but I didn't look up at him. I was fairly done with this conversation. I began to pick at the bottom of my shirt.

"You look cute when you're sad."

My eyes snapped up to his.

"Ask me another question." He tilted his head.

But I wasn't into games like this. I didn't flirt with strangers.

And even though I was participating reluctantly, I still felt like it was illegal.

Christian stretched his arms over his head and then exhaled. "Fine, I'll answer the one I'm sure you're dying to know."

"And which one is that?"

He widened his eyes as if it was a stupid question. "Whether or not I have a girlfriend."

There was an uneasy turn to my stomach. No. Actually, I hadn't been wondering that, but if he did have a girlfriend, I would be very disappointed. I wasn't sure Kira could take another heartbreak.

"You look worried, Tessa," he said, completely misreading my expression. "I don't have a girlfriend. I don't even have a psychotic ex. So you're in the clear."

Me? Why was I in the clear? Maybe I needed to be more direct.

"Christian," I said simply, touching his arm. He flexed. "Christian, I'm not sure if this is accidental or not, but it seems like you're hitting on me." My face was beginning to redden. This was much easier to say in my head. I dropped my hand.

"It is accidental," he said smiling, looking embarrassed. I sighed with relief. He leaned closer to me. "I wasn't supposed to *seem* like I was. I am hitting on you."

Shake and bake!

"But . . . Kira . . ."

He pursed his lips. "To be honest, I'm not really into blondes. I like you."

"But . . . why?" What made him think that he was at all my type? He didn't even play a sport!

Christian adjusted in his seat and looked thoughtfully at me. "You're just different. Sweet. Beautiful. You're . . . perfect. You're just perfect."

I swallowed hard. Was I perfect? Did he believe that? Did I?

There was a low whistle, and I looked toward the doorway out into the hallway. My chest swelled. Aiden. Like a tall drink of lemonade on a hot day, my guy stood there in a tracksuit with his hair a perfect mess. Thank goodness he was here. I knew he'd come for me.

He winked before striding into the classroom, pretending not to look my way. Christian groaned next to me. He might not be as elated as I was.

"Mr. Wilder," Mr. Powell said, sounding amused. "What can I do you for, son?" My teacher flicked his eyes to mine. I shrugged.

Aiden sounded sweet. "Sorry to bother you, sir, but Tessa has my lunch in her locker and I'm so hungry." He clutched his stomach. "We have practice after school, and if I don't get something to eat—"

Powell waved him off. "Just take her," he said. He looked at me. "Ms. Crimson, I expect you won't be late again?"

I smiled and shook my head. He motioned for the door. I jumped up, shooting Christian one last glance before walking away. He sucked at his teeth.

"See ya," he said. He looked up at Aiden. "Thanks for the invite, by the way."

Aiden raised his chin to him. "No problem, Chris. I'll see you Saturday." Then he held his hand out to me. I jogged up to take it, thrilled to finally see him. His fingers squeezed mine, and they were warm, protective. We began walking out.

"Cool," Christian called to us. "And it's Christian."

"Sorry," Aiden said, not looking back. "See you later, man." And we left.

I debated telling Aiden about Christian's failed attempt to woo me but decided it would only cause more friction. And friction was not something I needed. Not when I was overflowing with assignments.

The minute we got in the empty hall, I tugged on Aiden's hand. He looked down at me and batted his eyelashes dramatically. Wow. He looked fantastic, and my anxiety began to ease as I stared back at him.

"You missed me, didn't you?" he asked expectantly.

"Madly. Where were you?"

He let go of my hand and placed his arm over my shoulders as we headed down the empty hall to the cafeteria. We didn't need to go to my locker—Aiden never brought his lunch to school. That was just a lie to get me out of detention fifteen minutes early. He knew Mr. Powell would let me go because he was a huge supporter of the Wildcats. That man had spirit.

Aiden exhaled. "I got to school late because my mother was bitching me out about some stupid phone call she got last night."

"Phone call?"

"Yeah. Some asshole called her last night and said that I was fucking around after practice or something—"

I slapped him in the stomach. His language was atrocious today. "Sorry." He shook his head. "Well, anyway, they told her I was drinking and driving. So she took my car. She wouldn't even let me use the phone to call you."

I stopped walking, letting his arm fall off of me. "What in heaven's name? Who would do that?"

"Seriously," he agreed. "I wouldn't drink after practice, and I definitely wouldn't drive if I did."

As I stared up at Aiden, my heart was racing. Nobody messed with him like that. Aiden was very well liked. Ping-Pong and pogo sticks! This was weird.

"Do you think . . ." I paused. I didn't want to say it.

"Christian?" he asked for me.

I twitched my nose, sort of embarrassed for accusing without evidence. That was not the SOS way.

"Already thought of that," Aiden said, reaching out to put his arms around my waist to pull me to him. "But my mom said it was a girl."

My mouth fell open. Oh, I did not like that. Not at all. "A girl?" It came out as a squeak. My fur prickled. Aiden's mother probably loved that. Someone other than me calling the house.

"Aw, baby," he said, and chuckled. "They were throwing me under the bus, not asking me out." He bent down and kissed my forehead. "Retract the claws."

I swatted him and backed up. "Well, I still don't like it," I said.

"Yeah, me either. I'm not allowed to have the car for a week."

Jeez Louise! That was harsh. "I'll drive you," I said, taking his hand and tugging him down the stairs to the cafeteria. I was still starving.

"Thank God she's gone this weekend," Aiden said, lifting my fingers to his mouth to kiss them.

Right, I had a question about that. "Why did you invite Chloe?" I asked, not turning around. I didn't want to tell him I'd forgotten about his party, even though I wasn't entirely sure he'd told me about it.

"Who's Chloe?"

"Christian's sister." I smiled a little. I was happy to hear that he didn't recognize her name. Even though she was clearly hunting him.

"Oh, her," he said, pausing for a minute. "I just invited both of them to be nice."

I twirled to face him as we entered the cafeteria doors. "To be nice?"

"Yeah, baby. I wanted to be polite. I knew you'd like it." He made a face like that was the only obvious answer, even though I was sure my Wildcat wasn't *that* polite.

"Wow," I said, pretending to take the bait. "That sure is sweet of you."

"I know." He widened his eyes, mocking our conversation, and puckered his lips like he wanted a kiss. I had narrowed my eyes, ready to argue, when I caught sight of Chloe over his shoulder, sitting at our lunch table. She glanced up at us, and I felt a rush of possessiveness.

"Come here," I purred at Aiden, taking a fistful of his shirt and pulling him toward me. Aiden looked down at me knowingly.

"Mm . . . my kitty's feeling frisky."

I laughed, letting my anger melt away.

Aiden leaned all the way down to pause his lips just above mine. "You're going to stay this weekend, right?"

I met his green gaze, and my insides began to liquefy like they always did when Aiden looked at me like that. I nodded. He grinned and then pressed his warm mouth to mine, squeezing me tight. When we parted, he winked at me.

"Now let's get you fed," he said. "You need to store up some energy."

He was so steamy.

When we got to our table, Chloe was gone. Her much-needed absence totally released the tension I'd been holding in my shoulders all day. Aiden went up to the line and grabbed me a lunch tray filled with hot sliced turkey. Then he excused himself to go over some plays with his team. It was perfect timing. It left me alone with my squad. The minute he walked away, we all leaned into the Formica table in unison.

"What's the double scoop?" I asked, setting down my spork and looking between their faces.

Leona adjusted her glasses. "Three assignments. Two cheater requests and a background check. And since two of our Kittens, Melody and Frances, went out of town this week, I'm not sure we have the cheer power to complete them."

Hm. Leona had a good point. We were down four pom-poms.

"I miss them," Izzie said, wiping her nose. "I hope they come back soon."

Leona shook her head. "Get focused, girls. We're not going to let these cheaters get the best of us. We may be outnumbered, but they're outsmarted. Tess, you have a plan, right?"

Her question caught me off guard. Although I knew my squad would be short a few members, I hadn't made a plan B. I wasn't even sure I had a plan A.

"Of course Tessa has a plan," Kira said, annoyed with Leona's question.

I looked between all of their trusting eyes and began to feel something. Panic. But I cleared my throat and channeled the SOS ways. "Kira," I said in my captain voice, "you and Izzie focus on the first cheater request. Stake out with visual only."

She smiled. "On it, Tess."

"Leona, you and Kara map out the second request, and we'll set it up for Wednesday night." I snapped my fingers. "Oh, and Leona, I need you to update the Naughty List and return some of those texts. Sound good?" Phew.

Leona stared at me. "What about the background check?"

Oh. I'd forgotten one. How did I . . . "Um . . . I'll do that one. Just forward me the information." I was confused.

Leona twisted her adorable necklace around her finger. "Tessa, it's your night with the SOS phone. You know that, right?"

I didn't.

"I'm going to use it tonight," Kira interrupted. "I already cleared it with Tess." She looked across the table and smiled encouragingly at me. She'd just saved my rep. That girl rocked.

"Great," Leona mumbled, resting her chin on her upturned palm. "Another night of texts from Kira. Just don't send me any more pictures of guys' butts, okay?"

Kira grinned. "If I can help it. But you did see Maxwell, right?"

"I know." Izzie giggled next to her. "It was nice. How about Jonathon Stuart . . ."

The girls began to talk among themselves about the best backsides in the junior class. I would have loved to listen to the conversation, but I was too busy staring at Aiden across the lunchroom.

He was laughing, joking with Darren and the guys. Then suddenly, he looked up and saw me watching. He smiled and winked. It made me uneasy, seeing how well my boyfriend fit in with a table of cheaters. I pushed the thought away.

Still, it made me think of Chloe and the fact that she was going after my boyfriend so obviously. And I certainly didn't like the way she searched me, looking for my cracks. In fact, I wished the little blond temptress would transfer to another school altogether.

But I didn't get my wish.

Chloe joined us for lunch the next day, clad in a super-tight pair of jeans and a baby tee. The Smitten Kittens had put aside their dislike for her earlier comments toward me once she'd apologized. They were such good sports. But I wasn't going to be so forgiving. At least not on the inside.

But I was surprised and delighted to see that Christian looked like he was taking a shine to Kira. He'd even started sitting next to her. I mean, it was directly across from me but also next to Kira. And even though they didn't talk to each other, they both talked to me, which was also something they had in common.

A happy thought struck me. Aiden's party was this weekend, and it was only natural for new couples to form at a party. Even Romeo and Juliet met at a party. I could get Kira and Christian together. Maybe then he'd focus his attention elsewhere.

SOS
CHEATER INCIDENT REPORT

CASE: 004
CLIENT: Madeline Haskel
SUBJECT: Roger Stanvick

Dear Ms. Haskel,

SOS is happy to honor your Potential Boyfriend Background Check voucher. And although it's tragic that we've had to deliver bad news to you on three separate occasions, we hope that by providing you with this service, you can make an informed decision on your next choice of companionship.

Mr. Stanvick will be observed within 48 hours of this notification. Please remember that this voucher is only valid for one background check per semester.

Thank you for your referrals, and SOS truly hopes that your dating needs are met. If you need to cancel this assignment, please text the stop order form within 24 hours. Have a great day.

Keep smiling,
SOS
Text: 555-0101
Exposing Cheaters for Over Two Years

CHAPTER TEN

IT WAS GETTING LATE. I YAWNED.

"What was the ETA?" Leona asked. She stretched out across the backseat of my car, her dark hair spreading like a fan across the leather upholstery.

I leaned against the headrest. "An hour ago." Here we were, camped out in front of an all-night miniature golf course, and we couldn't even play. The parking lot was deserted, and the sky was nearly starless. There was little pep in this car.

Luckily this was a small assignment, only two Kittens needed. And Leona was the only one available to help me. I was very thankful. Alone, I might have fallen asleep.

We were on a potential boyfriend background check. We reserved that only for our repeat clients. It wasn't something I was proud of since officially, the clients weren't dating the suspects. But if SOS had investigated for them at least three times, the client was given a certificate for a complimentary background check. Hopefully it could save them future heartache.

"He works here, right?" Leona asked. Sometimes it was difficult being alone with her. She didn't have the perk that Kira did.

"Yep. And my informant said he was working ten to two this morning."

"It's after eleven."

"Thank you, Leona. I hadn't noticed."

"Whoa." She sat up, and I could feel her glare on the side of my face. I turned slowly to her.

"Sorry to snap," I said quietly. "I just want to go home."

Leona eyed me from behind her glasses. She was angry. She didn't like to be scolded or talked down to. And I should have controlled myself better. Being short-tempered just wasn't the Smitten Kitten way. I pursed my lips.

"Things have been getting harder," I said apologetically.

She nodded, her face clearing. "I know, Tess. And you've seemed, well a little distracted. Is everything okay with Aiden?"

My mouth opened. That was an unexpected question. "Of course. Why would you ask that?" My heart beat a little faster.

She shrugged. "I don't know. You two don't seem to be spending as much time together."

I blinked rapidly, a stabbing pain in my ribs. She was right. We hadn't. But Aiden had basketball, and I had cheerleading. Between that, I had SOS assignments. Lots of them. Oh, my word. Were we growing apart?

"Great Caesar's ghost! Give me your phone, Leona. Mine's dead." I needed to talk to Aiden. I needed to hear him.

Leona's eyes widened at my abrupt change in demeanor, but she pulled out her phone anyway. "I'll be outside with the binoculars," she said cautiously.

I waited until she got out into the parking lot and shut the door before punching in the numbers. "Pick up, Aiden," I whispered, glancing at the dashboard clock.

"Hello." Shoot. Mrs. Wilder.

"Hi, it's Tessa." For the first time, my voice wasn't dripping with sweetness. I just wanted to talk to her son. "Can I speak with Aiden, please? It's important."

"He's not with you?"

My stomach dropped. "What?"

"Aiden's not here, Tessa. I thought he was out with you tonight."

I was shaking my head, even though I knew she couldn't see me. "No . . . I'm . . . I'm not with him."

"Huh."

That was it? That was all she had to say? I tried to take a deep breath, but I was having trouble breathing. What was going on? Where was my sweetie?

"Tell him I called," I murmured and hung up. I couldn't stick around and wait for any of her snide remarks. My eyes stung, and I sat up straighter to check my reflection in the rearview mirror. I was surprised to see that a little bit of my mascara had smeared. I wiped it quickly. What else could go wrong?

There was a knock on my driver's side window, and I nearly jumped out of my skin. I turned, my hand at my throat.

Christian was bent down, looking in. He waved. What in the world?

I turned my key in the ignition to get power and lowered the window, my brow furrowed. "Christian?"

"Hi, Tessa." He smiled. "I thought this was your car."

I took in a sharp breath. How did he know my car?

He chuckled, pushing his hair behind his ears. "Sorry, that sounds sort of stalkerish, right?"

It definitely did, but I was too stunned to nod. Wait. I was on assignment. He'd now caught me twice on assignment. Not good.

"Um . . . what do you want?" It wasn't a polite question, but it needed to be asked.

He grinned, as if he had a dirty joke waiting. Thankfully, he decided to act appropriately. "I was just wondering why you were parked in the back lot. And why your friend was watching the course with binoculars." He tilted his head. "Are you guys spying on someone?"

Cracker Jacks! "No. That's a silly question."

He narrowed his eyes, studying me. "Is it?"

I stared back at him, speechless, as the wind blew around his chocolate hair. He really was attractive. Not *Aiden* cute, but still handsome. I swallowed hard.

"Are you here alone?" I asked. A subject change was in order.

"Nope."

I waited. When it became apparent that he wasn't going to volunteer the information, I pressed further. "Who are you with?"

He smiled. "Don't worry, I'm not on a date. I'm with Colton."

I made a face. I wasn't worried he was on a date. I just wanted him to trot away. "Wonderful." He didn't move.

"So," he said, looking around at the interior of my car. I was hyper-aware of the equipment on my passenger seat—the camera with tripod, the utility vest, and the grappling hook that Leona had wanted to bring (even though I was pretty sure we didn't need it). He glanced at it, then back at me. "No boyfriend tonight?"

My face stung. "Maybe later," I said. But it was probably a lie.

"Too bad." Christian straightened, sliding his hands into the pockets of his khakis. I looked for Leona, but she was sitting on a parking curb observing the course, clueless of the complication that was just outside my window.

"You and Leona want to join us for a round of golf?" Christian asked.

I turned back to him. "What?"

He leaned over, resting his forearms on my windowsill. I moved back in my seat. He was so different outside of school, much bolder. It scared me.

"You're here to play golf, right? Why else would you be here, Tessa?"

Holy cocker spaniel! Did he know? He was smirking, daring me to lie. My mouth felt suddenly dry; my stomach flipped.

"Come on," he whispered playfully. "I'll let you win."

Well, now that was condescending. "You wouldn't need to let me, Christian. I would beat you fair and square."

He laughed. *"Fair and square?* You are too cute. Seriously. I can't get enough of you."

I blinked quickly.

"Come play with me," he said, opening my door. "One round."

Did I have a choice? How odd would it look if we just left? I paused, trying to think of the possibly horrific outcomes that could come from this. But there wasn't time to think it through. I was the captain, and I was the one responsible for the tough decisions.

I took a breath. "Just one game," I said.

Christian held out his hand to me, but I looked at him like he'd lost his marbles. I certainly wasn't going to hold his hand. This wasn't a date and never would be. I was Aiden's girl.

My stomach turned. I just wished I knew where Aiden was.

Christian tried to win at miniature golf, but he had seriously underestimated my ball-sinking skills. He also found it hilarious

when I told him that. But he was polite. Sweet, even. And his friend
Colton seemed to warm to cheerleaders, especially dark-haired
ones named Leona. But I didn't forget that he had a girlfriend from
a rival school, and I made sure Leona didn't forget either.

At some point, one game turned into two. It was nearly one in
the morning when we walked back to my car, Leona giggling with
Colton behind me. The night had been fun. Completely unethical,
but fun. We paused at my car.

"Thanks for hanging out, Tessa," Christian said, stopping to
stand directly in front of me. His cologne was carrying in the wind,
and it smelled really fresh. Clean. Aiden didn't bother with cologne;
he smelled more athletic.

"Well," I said, darting a warning glance at Leona as she paused
alarmingly close to Colton. She nodded knowingly and dropped her
eyes. I turned back to Christian. "We've got to jet. I'll see you at
school on Monday."

He chuckled. "You're not going to your boyfriend's party
tomorrow?"

Sweet tea and honey! I'd forgotten again. "No, I'll be there."

"Cool," Christian said. "Then I'll see you there."

My face was burning with both embarrassment and shame. And
just then, Christian leaned toward me. Like toward my mouth!

I dodged quickly, trying not to make a complete spectacle, but
in my haste, I head-butted Christian in the jaw.

"Ow," we said at the same time. I put my palm against my
forehead, and he covered his mouth. Leona burst out laughing from
the other side of the car.

"You're a violent little thing, Tessa." He laughed and dropped
his hand, running his eyes slowly up and down my body. "I say you

ditch your jock and come wrestle with me sometime." He winked. "You can't always be good, right?"

I squeaked. Did he just tell me to break up with Aiden? Ew, did he just ask to *wrestle* with me? Without another word, I scrambled into the driver's seat and slammed the door.

Leona got in too, adjusting her glasses and turning to me with a smirk. "He's still staring," she sang. "He's, like, obsessed with you or something."

"Shoot. This was a really bad idea. We'll have to reschedule this mission for tomorrow night."

"Wait. Do you think he knows we're SOS?" Her face was worried.

"Let's hope not."

Ignoring Christian, still standing outside my window, I started my car and pulled quickly out of the parking lot, squealing my tires.

I dropped Leona off at her grandmother's, and when I got home, the house was dark. My parents must still be at the club.

I felt lonely. I'd been hoping to sit down and talk with my dad while we had milk and cookies, but he wasn't here. I needed advice. I wanted him to tell me that I had nothing to worry about.

At 2 a.m., my cell rang. I reached over to pluck it off my side table, but I didn't recognize the number. I squashed my panic and answered.

"Hello?" *Please don't be Christian.*

"Hi, baby," Aiden said in a deep, tender voice.

I exhaled, pulling the phone into my sheets as I curled up with it, comforted by Aiden's sound. I'd missed the snot out of him.

"Where are you?" I asked, bringing my blankets up under my

chin. My chest was aching. I was so confused by our recent lack of cuddle time.

He chuckled. "I'm at your front door."

I smiled, my stomach knotting with excitement. "Really?"

"Yeah, really. Now come let me in."

I squealed and then clicked off the call. Throwing back my sheets, I jumped out of bed and tossed my cell on it before dashing through the house barefoot.

I paused in front of my wood front door and then took a deep breath and swung it open. My face immediately brightened. There he was, leaning his long body against my door frame, his hair a mess of blond tangles. He was in a pair of jeans with a dark green sweater, making his eyes more noticeable than usual. He looked . . . fantastic.

"Hi," he said in that low, sexy voice.

"Hi."

We stood for a minute, staring at each other. My body was tingling, wanting him, but I knew that we should probably talk first. A breeze blew past him from outside. I twitched my nose.

"Are . . . are you wearing cologne?" I asked.

He grinned. "Uh, yeah. Why?"

"You don't wear cologne."

"I do sometimes."

"No. You don't."

Aiden furrowed his brow, pushing off the door to step inside the house, his dress shoes making a different noise on the tile than his sneakers normally did. He paused in front of me and looked down.

"What's wrong?" he asked, studying my face.

"Where were you?"

Aiden turned and shut the door, then came back and reached out to push my hair over my shoulder before resting his hand there.

"Darren was dealing with some shit. I went over to help him out."

"Wearing cologne?"

Aiden stepped back from me, looking a little annoyed. "Tess, are you pissed at me or something? What's with the cologne? Do you not like it?"

My fingers trembled. Aiden never got annoyed with me. I was . . . losing it a little. It was SOS. It was making me suspicious of my sweetie. But I knew better. Aiden would never hurt me. He wasn't like those other guys.

"I'm sorry," I said, swallowing hard and walking up to slide my arms around his waist. I laid my head against his chest but felt uneasy when he didn't squeeze me the way I'd expected him to. "Whose phone do you have?" I asked.

"Borrowed Darren's." Aiden's fingers slowly traced up my spine, feeling it through my silk pajama top. But when he got to my shoulders, he braced me and held me back to look at my face. He stared at me for a minute, his eyes uneasy. Then he pulled me gently into a hug and rested his chin on top of my head. "I missed you, baby," he murmured. "Didn't you miss me?"

Did he feel it too? The strangeness of us? "I always miss you," I breathed.

He shifted, pressing closer to me, clearly liking my answer. "I can't stay tonight," he said.

My stomach turned. "Oh."

"But I'll give you a foot rub before I leave," he whispered seductively.

Was that it? Was he just here to hook up? I pulled back from him, my eyes beginning to tear.

"What?" he asked, looking alarmed.

"You came here for that?"

"For what? Tessa, what is going on? You're seriously freaking me out." Aiden put his palms on my cheeks, watching as a few tears trickled down them. "Tell me what's wrong."

But I couldn't. How could I tell him that SOS had trained me to scout out cheaters, and now he was showing the classic signs? How could I say that to the guy I loved?

"It's nothing," I said, sniffling. "Just tuck me in, okay?"

I thought Aiden might cry too. He looked so frustrated. Helpless. So I just took his hand, kissed it, and then held it in my own as I pulled him toward my bedroom.

SOS
CHEATER INCIDENT REPORT

CASE: 050

CLIENT: Desiree Tucker

SUBJECT: Rueben Monroe

FINDINGS: At approximately 7:30 a.m. on February 28, Mr. Monroe was observed getting out of the car of a person other than the client in front of Washington High. It was later determined that the driver was his mother, Claire Monroe. She looks very young for her age.

However, Mr. Monroe was picked up from the building by a different vehicle. The car was registered to a Mrs. Yvonne Gallagher, his mother's best friend. Mr. Monroe and Mrs. Gallagher were followed back to her house on Sycamore Drive, where the enclosed photos were taken. You will notice that they confirm sexual intercourse.

Phone records also indicate a consistent relationship dating back several months, or since Mr. Monroe turned eighteen. It is our determination that the subject is cheating.

We trust that this report will remain confidential as some of the information contained within could compromise our top-secret status.

SOS is sorry for your loss, and we offer our deepest sympathies. We hope that we will not have to assist you again in the future, but please keep us in mind for referrals.

Keep smiling,

SOS
Text: 555-0101

Exposing Cheaters for Over Two Years

CHAPTER ELEVEN

LOW-KEY? AIDEN HAD TOLD ME HE'D KEEP THE party low-key. Hm. Was that why half of the graduating class was having a bonfire in his backyard barbecue pit? There had to be close to a hundred and fifty people here! And even though Aiden's grassy yard was great for playing volleyball in the summer, right now it was scattered with red plastic cups and cigarette butts. His mother would flip if she saw that.

Inside, Aiden's professionally decorated house had become a mass of jocks, cheerleaders, and upperclassmen. In fact, most of his furniture was pushed to the wall to make a dance floor. I kept my eye on the entrance waiting to see who else would show.

Just then another group came in the door, and my heart skipped a beat. Christian and Chloe. Chloe saw me immediately and smiled. I was ashamed to admit that I was a little jealous. Her long blond hair was pretty, blown out pin straight and smooth. Her frayed denim miniskirt and braless tank top were way more revealing than anything non-uniformed I'd wear. But she wore it well. She looked very desirable.

I glanced around for Aiden. He was in the corner by the pool table, watching Darren tell an animated basketball story. At least it looked like a basketball story. Not sure what else those hip-thrusting movements could stand for.

"Ew," Leona said, coming to stand next to me. "*She* showed up."
I grinned before looking sideways at her. Leona's hair was in a high
ponytail, and she had extra-big hoops in her ears. She was super-
stylish. Just then Kira came bouncing over, nodding emphatically
as she snapped her gum.

"Well, well," she said, blowing a bubble and then sucking it in
with a loud pop.

"Chloe's outfit is totally tawdry. She reminds me of that Yvonne
lady that Rueben Monroe's been doing."

"She does!" Leona said, turning to her and laughing.

Even though I was happy to see Leona and Kira getting along
for once, talking so carelessly about a scandal was hardly becoming
of a Smitten Kitten.

"We don't discuss assignments outside of practice," I said
quietly, leaning back on my heels as I spoke.

"Sorry," they both mumbled.

"Besides," I said, looking worriedly at Chloe. "We really
should be more polite." I folded my hands behind my back, wishing
Christian's sister would change her mind and leave.

Kira stepped forward, fluffing her curls, and then turned back
to me, grinning. "For sure, Tessa. It *is* the Smitten Kitten way."
She winked and walked through the crowded room, looking perkier
than usual, her pink skirt fluttering up with her movements.

"Uh-oh," Leona said. "Seems she's found her next victim."
Guess their truce hadn't lasted long.

I was about to scold Leona for picking on Kira again, but she
turned to leave before I could. Then Kira's high-pitched voice
carried over the crowd.

"Hi, Christian," she said with exaggerated enthusiasm, putting her
arms around his waist and hugging him. Chloe shot her a dirty look.

"Oh," Christian said, looking surprised by her attention. "What's up, Kira?" He shot a quick look around, found me, and then went back to staring at her.

"Chloe," Kira said, turning to her, just as loudly. "I'm so glad you're here."

Christian's sister seemed thrown off. "Me . . . too?"

Kira giggled, releasing her grip on Christian to embrace his sister. I snickered. Chloe looked freaked out by Kira's hospitality. My counselor had once told me that children of divorce sometimes lack self-esteem. Hm. I might have believed that about Chloe if she weren't scouting the room, totally looking for my boyfriend.

"Let me show you around," Kira said, taking her by the elbow. "Aiden's pretty busy."

Nice. Kira was a clever Kitten sometimes. The last thing I wanted was for my boyfriend to give Chloe a personal tour. Not when she was dressed like that. I looked back for Aiden, but he was gone. My stomach turned.

"Hi, Tessa."

I jumped. Christian. "Hi." Dang. He always snuck up on me.

"You look beautiful," he said. "That dress is really pretty." I smiled. It was nice of him to notice my outfit. I thought a sundress was perfectly suited. For a *low-key* party!

"Thanks," I responded. "You look peachy too." And he did. Nice button-down, loafers, hair pulled back in a ponytail. Very preppy cute.

We stood for a minute, awkwardly, as someone got ahold of the stereo and began blasting it with full bass. Christian stepped over to me and leaned his head next to mine to talk. "Tessa, do you know where the beer is?"

"Yeah." I nodded.

"Will you show me? I'm feeling a little nervous." He paused, and his dark eyes looked different. Anxious.

Balderdash! If he was feeling so uneasy, I must not be acting as a very gracious hostess. Just then someone turned down the music, and I took a deep breath. I didn't like having to shout when I wasn't in the gymnasium.

I shook my long waves to clear my head, about to cross the room. "I'm so sorry," I said to Christian. "I'll get you one—"

"I'll come with you," he interrupted, stepping up and looping his arm in mine.

My smile faded. "I—"

"I'm back," Kira announced as she bounded next to me. She was grinning from ear to ear, mostly at Christian. I exhaled. Thank heavens she'd come. Things had been getting very uncomfortable around here. I unwound his arm from mine.

"I've got to find Aiden," I said quickly, turning before I could see either of their expressions. Maybe leaving them alone together could spark something. I didn't need to tell Kira how Christian had been so forward with me; it might hurt her ego. And I didn't want to do that—not when Christian was clearly misguided in his feelings for me.

I was standing next to Darren, but my boyfriend was no longer here. Darren turned to me, a pool stick in his hand. "Hey there, Sex Kitten," he said in his smooth, deep voice. "You hunting for your boy?"

"It's Smitten. And yes, have you seen him?" I put my fists on my hips, feeling a bit lost.

"Yeah." He pointed toward the back door. "He went out to the bonfire to get more beers. Tell him to hurry up, will ya, Tess?"

"Sure."

I chewed on my lip as I made my way through the kitchen to the yard. The music was louder out here with the bass pumping through the speakers set up on the patio. Luckily Aiden's nearest neighbor was half an acre away. Besides, there was no need to worry about getting in trouble. No one would call the police on the Wildcats' point guard—we had a chance to make the playoffs this year!

I paused as I stepped onto his wooden deck. Aiden was in the grass at the keg, laughing, smiling, and looking very happy . . . talking with Chloe. My face stung. She tossed her blond hair over her shoulder, and as she bent down in front of Aiden to get a plastic cup out of its sleeve, her cleavage was on full display. I think I even saw a nipple. Aiden looked away quickly. He must have too.

I put my palm over my forehead, feeling sick. Backing up, I turned around and walked into the house. It was loud. People were talking, saying hi to me as I moved past them. I found a quiet spot against the wall in the hallway near the stairs. My heart was racing.

Nothing was going on with Aiden and Chloe. I was being irrational. He was just talking to her—probably being polite, like I'd always told him to be. I needed to get a grip. I closed my eyes.

A few minutes passed, but I didn't move. I didn't want to go back out there. I didn't want to see if it had gotten any worse.

"You okay?" Christian was next to me, talking in a soft voice. I couldn't look at him. But I felt him lean next to me against the wall.

"Fine."

"You don't look like you're having very much fun."

I opened my eyes and turned to him. He smiled and took a sip from the cup of beer he was holding. That was an understatement.

I nodded. "Yeah, it's been a weird night."

"I know. Me too."

I tilted my head. "Why is it weird for you?"

"Kira. You trying to leave us alone together." He chuckled. "Very slick," he added sarcastically.

That was funny. I'd actually thought it *was* sort of slick. I glanced down the hall, back to where the party was in full force, wondering what Aiden was doing.

"Your boyfriend is ignoring you," Christian said, staring into his beer.

My stomach dropped. "Excuse me?"

Christian's eyes met mine, looking at me in the aggressive way they had that night at miniature golf.

"He is ignoring you, isn't he?"

"No."

"In fact, I think he's talked to Chloe more than he's talked to you tonight."

"Well, then maybe you should grab your sister and go," I snapped. My breath caught. I couldn't believe I was being so rude! What was happening to me?

"Naw." Christian shook his head. "I don't tell my sister what to do. She can handle herself. She always has." Christian looked me up and down. "And right about now, I think she wants to handle your boyfriend."

I was about to raise my voice or push him violently. Do *something*. But I just stared at him, my chest heaving under my sundress. Did he think Aiden liked her?

Christian looked away, almost like he was sorry he'd brought it up, but I doubted he was. He probably saw it as an opening to get to me. It wasn't.

"Can I grab you a beer?" he asked.

I shook my head, still trying to understand the jealousy raging through me. "No, thank you."

Christian chuckled. "Let me guess—you don't drink either?"

"Nope." It wasn't like I'd never had alcohol before; I just preferred not to drink it on a regular basis. But honestly, a beer didn't sound like a bad idea right now.

Christian took a long sip from his cup, smiling to himself. "You are definitely nothing like the other cheerleaders I've met."

I was about to be offended on behalf of all spirit saviors everywhere when Christian reached out, touching one of the thick waves of hair that hung over my shoulder. I gasped. He wasn't allowed to touch me. Even my hair. And he shouldn't be caressing my strands like that!

"Hey there, Chris," Aiden called out as he appeared behind him. He stepped forward, dropping his heavy arm over Christian's shoulders.

Christian's face fell, and he immediately unhanded my hair. He nodded at Aiden, looking uncomfortable, and then took a nervous sip from his drink.

My face tingled as my eyes met Aiden's slightly glassy gaze. I had nothing to be ashamed of—it wasn't like I'd forced my hair in between Christian's fingers—but I felt a little guilty. SOS tendency. Non-boyfriend physical contact was a definite no-no.

Aiden beamed at me, taking a drink from his own beer. He looked sideways at Christian. "Is Tessa being a good hostess?" he asked, pulling him into one of those almost headlock hugs and releasing him with a laugh.

I blinked rapidly, trying to read Aiden's mood. He looked fine. A little drunk, but otherwise stellar.

"Yeah," Christian said, straightening his shirt before looking back at my boyfriend. "Tessa's being very polite."

Normally I'd have thought it was sweet of him to notice, but right now, I wasn't in the mood. I wanted to talk to Aiden.

My boyfriend looked proud. "Tessa is always nice, aren't you, baby? Especially to strangers." He set his beer on the hallway table and stepped forward, putting his hand in my hair and holding a few strands there, palm up, like he was checking to see if Christian had damaged it.

"A little ray of sunshine," he continued, separating the strands with his fingers. I could smell the alcohol on his breath. "Did you miss me?" he asked, meeting my eyes and then narrowing his seductively.

I nodded, suddenly and completely hot for him, hotter than usual. Was it the way he was touching me? Was it Christian or his sister? I wasn't sure. But I licked my lips, daring Aiden to be naughty. He noticed.

He slid his hand over my shoulder and behind my neck to draw me against him. But instead of ravaging me, he leaned over to kiss my cheek lightly, pausing there to whisper, "You're my little angel, Tessa Crimson." When he pulled away, we stood there watching each other, both of us breathing a little heavy.

Christian coughed.

My boyfriend exhaled and straightened up, taking a second to look down at me adoringly. "I love you," he mouthed silently before bending back down to peck my lips.

"I love you too." I didn't bother whispering it. I wanted the world to know.

"You continue being cute," he said to me, raising his eyebrow. "But not too cute." He smiled, and I felt decidedly better.

"I'll try," I said.

"Now I'm going downstairs to the basement to watch the game

on the big screen with the team. Unless, of course, you needed to talk to me alone, Tessa." His eyes flashed wickedly.

He made my insides turn to oatmeal when he talked sexy like that. "I think we can chat later." We'd have to. Hooking up at a party full of people would be a terrible example to set.

"Oh, we can," Aiden agreed, nodding, slowly backing up. "And I have *a lot* to say, too. It's going to be a very *long* conversation."

"Good."

"Good."

I smiled as I watched Aiden walk toward the stairs. Then, as if in afterthought, he turned around. "Don't keep her too long, Chris. Tessa has other guests to be polite to."

"It's Christian," Christian said, mostly under his breath.

Aiden winked at me and then disappeared down the steps. Feeling much better, I watched as the rest of the team filed down after him. I was Aiden's angel! Everything was going to be fine.

"Tessa?"

I looked at Christian dreamily and wondered why he was still standing there. "What?"

"I know about you and SOS."

My. Heart. Stopped.

A breath escaped between my lips, but I couldn't speak. It was like my air was gone. Christian and I stared at each other, and he looked almost apologetic. But he knew. Leaping lizards! *He knew.*

"Let's go," a low voice hissed. I looked to my left to see Chloe approaching, a scowl firmly planted on her overly painted mouth.

I was shaking so badly, I was afraid I might pass out. I steadied myself against the wall. Christian reached out and put his hand on my waist.

"Hey," he whispered. "I'm sorry if I scared you. I promise I'm not going to tell anybody, but I think we should talk about it."

Keep breathing, Tessa.

"I'll see you later, okay?" And he did look sorry. That meant that he was either actually sorry or I was incredibly pale and he thought I might faint. Maybe both.

I glanced at Chloe. Her eyebrows were pulled together, but she didn't look too concerned with me. She was ticked about something else entirely. I wondered if it had to do with Aiden.

Christian was still touching me, and there was a sick turn in my belly. What now? Was he going to expose us? Try and blackmail me? I backed away from him, letting his hand fall.

He nodded, almost like he understood my dread. Then he turned around, took his sister by the elbow, and walked through the party and out the front door.

When he was gone, I ran to the bathroom and threw up.

"You're awfully quiet," Aiden said, kissing my neck as we lay together on the leather sofa in his basement. Normally I'd have made a squeak or two by now (he found that adorable), but my body was too numb. I was still in shock.

"Tessa," he mumbled, running his hand down to the bottom of my dress, tugging at my hem like he was dying to pull it off. "You're a bit . . . unresponsive, baby." He nibbled at my ear.

This could have been a good night. It felt like Aiden and I were getting back on track; and now, suddenly, the whole flipping train had derailed. And I didn't know where I was stranded.

"Sorry," I said, shifting my position under him, trying to refocus on the task at hand.

Aiden pulled my knee over his hip as he brought his mouth to mine again, kissing me deeply. But all I could think about were the Smitten Kittens. We'd lose everything. If everyone found out that we were SOS, we'd be shunned from high school society. Oh, my word. We'd be dead meat.

My boyfriend pulled away, breathing heavily, staring down into my face. I realized I wasn't panting at all. That might have hurt his ego.

"Tessa? What's up?"

He was still on top of me, but there was nothing frisky going on anymore. Aiden looked pretty annoyed as he tried to catch his breath.

I wanted to trust him with our secret. I wanted so much to be free of it, but what if he couldn't forgive me for lying to him? What would I do then?

"Nothing's wrong," I said quickly. Lincoln Memorial! All I did was lie.

Aiden stared at me before clenching his jaw and climbing off. He leaned over the edge of the sofa, putting his elbows on his knees and resting his head in his palms. He looked dejected.

"Aiden?"

He turned to me, his green eyes glassy but not from alcohol.

"I don't understand you anymore, Tess," he said seriously.

"Don't say that."

"It's true." He rubbed roughly at his face. "You're so distant. Distracted. Half the time, I don't even know if you're listening to me."

"Sweetie, I always listen . . ."

Aiden raked his fingers through his hair, staring across the room, pressing his lips together like he was trying to stop them from trembling. "Tessa," he said, sounding miserable. "Maybe my mother's right. Maybe we should—"

I jumped forward and grabbed his face, kissing him hard. I didn't want to know what he was about to say. There was nothing to talk about. There was nothing I *could* talk about. He just had to understand how much I needed him. Wanted him.

"Baby," he breathed, tangling his hand in my hair. "We don't have to . . ."

But I pushed him back on his couch, and we hooked up right here, in his basement. Without talking.

Aiden exhaled, snuggling closer to me, his face resting against the back of my neck. "I love you," he said.

I smiled. "I love you too." We were quiet for a minute, our heartbeats mixing together. I bit the inside of my cheek. Right now, I felt safe being here with him, so warm. At times like this, I felt like I could talk to him about anything—even SOS.

"Why did you invite Christian and Chloe to your party?" I asked. My boyfriend was the biggest sweetheart in the world, but he wasn't dense. If I knew about Christian's interest in me, Aiden had probably read it even sooner. So why would he invite him here?

Aiden sighed. "I'm not telling you. You'll be mad at me."

I rubbed my back into him, letting him wrap me up tighter. "I won't," I whispered. "I promise."

"I . . . thought he should know."

I scrunched my nose. "What did you need him to know?"

"That you're with me."

Talking about Christian was making me tremble. Did Aiden feel it? "He knows I'm with you," I said, but my voice cracked.

"Does he?"

I didn't like Aiden's tone. My paws had no intention of wandering anywhere else. "Yeah."

"Because by the way he was playing with your hair, Tess, he didn't seem to get the picture at all."

My face stung. Was he accusing me of something? I sat up, letting Aiden's arm fall off of me. "What are you saying?" I asked, glaring at him.

He scoffed. "I'm not a chump. The kid watches your ass every time you walk by. You telling me you haven't noticed?" Aiden pulled himself up, and I wished he'd put his shirt back on. It was very distracting when I was trying to be royally PO'd at him.

"I'm aware that Christian has a crush on me," I said. "But I'm trying to fix him up with Kira." Though now I had to rethink that. We'd all been compromised.

Aiden grabbed his T-shirt off the back of the couch and slid it over his head, pushing his arms roughly through the sleeves. "And how long have you been *aware* of it, Tessa?"

I tilted my head. It was nice to see Aiden get jealous, but I didn't need him to be unreasonable either. I'd still have to handle Christian somehow without exposing the Smitten Kittens. I straightened my posture. "At lunch detention he made it clear. And at miniature golf—"

"Wait. What?"

Gingersnaps! I'd let that one slip out.

"It was nothing." I waved my hand. "Leona and I—"

"Did you go on a fucking date with him?" Aiden's voice boomed through the room, bouncing off the cement walls of the basement. My face burned with shame.

"Absolutely not! How could you ask that?"

"I don't know, Tess. I never know where you are anymore. You're quiet all the time. You're like a different fucking person lately. . . ."

My mouth fell open. He was being crude.

"And don't tell me not to swear," he said, holding up a finger. "I'm really angry, and I have every right to swear."

"Aiden." I reached out to touch his hair, but he moved his head away.

"Would you rather I didn't give a shit? Would that be better?"

"No!" Hadn't I wanted Aiden to get a little jealous? He should be. Christian was after me. But I had to diffuse this situation because now, Christian had the power to ruin my life. To ruin Aiden and me.

I twitched my nose, trying to channel the sweet, peppy cheerleader everyone loved so much. I met Aiden's eyes.

"Forget Christian," I said in the cutest voice possible. "You're more than I can handle, Wildcat. And you're the only one I purr for." I leaned toward him and kissed his cheek, believing my words.

"Tessa," he whispered, but I could tell he liked it. He liked me like this.

"Come on, point guard," I said, standing up, taking his hand. "It's late. And I think my feet are still a little sore from practice. You . . ." I licked my lips. "You want to rub them for me?"

It was true. My toes did feel a little cramped, and Aiden liked to make them feel better. I'd deal with Christian later. Right now, I had someone else to cheer up. I could be like this. Energetic. Positive. Even if I was so very tired.

Aiden got up, looking at me doubtfully. Then, "Did you bring any polish?" he asked off-handedly, like he didn't care either way.

"Passion pink."

He growled. "Baby, that's my favorite."

"I know."

We stood together, smiling at each other, and it felt right. The way it'd been before SOS started getting so many cases. The times before new students came to Washington High to mess with my life.

Aiden and I were the real deal. We could get past this. If we loved each other, we could get past anything.

SOS
BACKGROUND CHECK RESULTS FORM

RESULT: 004
CLIENT: Madeline Haskel
SUBJECT: Roger Stanvick

Dear Ms. Haskel,

We are sorry to inform you that Mr. Stanvick's background report has not ended positively. SOS does not endorse him as your next boyfriend.

It was determined that Mr. Stanvick spent his 10 p.m. to 2 a.m. shift in Mini-Golf Mania's back room with an unidentified accomplice. We believe his name was Mark.

We are terribly sorry that it's not better news. SOS would like to offer you an extension on your certificate. Please let us know if you find another potential boyfriend. But we do advise that for your next subject, try to avoid the drama club.

Thank you for your continued support, and SOS truly hopes that your dating needs are eventually met. Have a great day.

Keep smiling,
SOS
Text: 555-0101
Exposing Cheaters for Over Two Years

CHAPTER TWELVE

ON SUNDAY, KIRA SHOWED UP WITH THE BLUE-prints for the next assignment. She'd spent half the day in the library while she mapped out Mitch Angley's house and charted our course. It was a rough one. Scaling walls, roof tie-downs. I hated second-story bedrooms.

I debated telling her about Christian, but Kira would get really shaky. That wouldn't work if she was going to be supporting my weight as I snapped some photos. No. This was my problem to handle. After all, I was the captain.

The night was quiet and cool as I started descending the wall of Mitch's house. The siding was slippery under my sneaks, and I tried my best to get a foothold.

"Tessa," Kira whispered from the roof above me. "I'm losing my grip."

Not good. If Kira (a very dependable base) did indeed lose her grip, I would end up in a pile on Mitch Angley's rosebushes. Ouch.

"Just one more second," I whispered. Placing my feet against the sill of Mitch's second-story bedroom window, I tried to take some of my weight off of Kira's short and compact frame.

I reached into my backpack, glancing down once to see that I would probably miss the rosebushes and instead land on the side yard fence. Silk pajamas! That would be painful.

"Hurry," Kira grunted, the rope shaking under my weight.

I found the night scope for my camera and snapped it on. It didn't take me long to find the figures in the dark room. Through the slats in the blinds, I aimed my camera at the bed. I swallowed the metallic taste in my mouth. There were some things a lady should never do, and one of them was to see another girl on her hands and knees and take a picture.

My stomach turned with anxiety. This was the part of the investigation I hated. The actual witnessing. It was worse than relaying the bad news, in truth because the bad news didn't come directly from me. In fact, Leona wrote up all the reports. But this, out here, hanging from a bungee on the side of Mitch Angley's house—this was me.

I snapped a few pictures, careful to make sure the shots would show their faces. It was a bit difficult at first, but thankfully, they eventually switched positions. After my last picture, I had turned to slide my camera into my backpack when I felt the first tug. I nearly dropped the camera.

"Kira," I whispered. Thank goodness Mitch's parents invested in those double-pane windows. The added sound barrier was essential right now, since getting caught dangling would be a very bad idea.

"I'm trying," she grunted.

Suddenly, I dropped down about five feet. My backpack slid off my shoulders and landed on the bushes below. Huh. I guessed I could make the roses after all.

I looked up. I wanted Kira to ease me up or set me down, but . . . I wasn't even sure where she was anymore. And I was just swaying.

Glancing around as I spun, I tried to find something to grab onto, but I was too far off the house now. I was afraid to swing on the rope because it might cause her to further lose her grip. Fiddler on the roof! I was going to break my leg.

"Drop down," a voice whispered from below me. My eyes widened.

"Christian?" This could not be happening. I was so busted. Christian had concrete proof now. I looked down at him and he smiled. He was wearing a black beanie and a dark, long-sleeved tee. Was he in disguise too?

"Hurry up." He laughed. "Just drop down. I've got you."

Got me? Hm. I didn't like the double meaning. Looking up the length of the rope, I considered trying to climb up it, but that was a physical fitness test that I had certainly failed. Rope climbing— not my thing.

"Tessa," Christian whispered loudly, holding his arms up like he would catch me. Not likely. I was still at least a dozen feet up.

"Kira," I called to the roof again. She squealed.

And then she dropped me.

"Holy shit," Christian said as I tumbled on top of him and, indeed he did *not* catch me. But he did break my fall.

We'd been loud. I saw the bedroom light flick on as Christian grabbed me by the sleeve and pulled me against the wall under the bedroom window. I was breathing heavily, terrified and still pumping adrenaline. I could hear Kira's sneakers scurry across the roof. Ouch. I might have sprained my ankle.

And there were Christian and I, panting, shoulder to shoulder against a house. I looked sideways at him.

"What are you doing here?" I whispered fiercely. He grinned.

"Saving your life." He looked away. "Obviously."

Well, that was sort of cute. But . . . peanut butter sandwiches! How did he find me? This was highly alarming.

I stepped away from the wall to glare at him. "Have you been following me?" Maybe that was how he'd found out about SOS in the first place. He was a flipping stalker!

"Following you?" he asked as if he didn't understand the question.

Oh, right. It was just a coincidence that he showed up, all covert-like.

The second-floor window slid open. My stomach dropped. Suddenly, Christian grabbed me around the waist and covered my mouth with his other hand, pulling me against him, pinning us to the wall.

Not good. We were pressed together, face to face, and I was unable to move. We listened, and Christian moved his hand away from my mouth, making my lips much more accessible to him. His breath smelled like spearmint. I narrowed my eyes.

"Who's out here?" Mitch called from the window.

Butterscotch! I pressed closer to Christian and tucked my head into his neck. He smelled really good. We couldn't get spotted now. Mitch was just above us. Christian's hand slid up my back to hold my neck under my hair protectively, inappropriately.

The night air was filled with the chirping of crickets, and I waited. I waited for the sound of the window, but all I could hear right now was the sound of my heartbeat pounding in my ears. I was in a very compromised position. And I did not like it.

There was a thump that I recognized as a pane closing, and I exhaled, straightening up. I looked up and saw the light flick out. Apple dippers! I thought I'd be against Christian for the rest of my life. I moved back, eyeing him.

He was smiling, no doubt still smelling my perfume. But he knew. Christian knew something about me that no one outside of the Smitten Kittens knew. Not even Aiden. We were spies. I'd have to find out how he'd compromised us, but first, I needed to skedaddle before Mitch found me hiding among his rosebushes.

"Now what?" I asked, jetting my glance around the property. My face was tingling. I hated that I needed to ask Christian anything, but I knew that boys didn't unmask a secret society of snooping cheerleaders, catch one falling off of a roof, and then just keep their mouths shut about it.

"We should get out of here," he said. "Let me take you home."

I groaned. Sure, it sounded simple, but this Kitten wasn't born yesterday. Christian wanted to offer me more than a ride home. Did I have a choice? That was the better question.

The SOS cell phone vibrated in my pocket. My eyes flicked to Christian's. He was grinning madly. I turned away and put the phone to my ear. It was Kira.

"Tess." She was frantic. "Oh, my, are you hurt?"

"I'm fine," I whispered, although my ankle did feel a little sore. "You guys go to Leona's, and I'll meet you there later."

"What?" She was freaked out. The second rule of SOS was never to leave a Smitten Kitten behind.

"It's okay," I said. "I have to take care of something. I'll see you in an hour."

I could sense her worry. Poor thing, she wasn't good at making split-second decisions—like that time she let Mike Rambler get to second base.

"K, I have to go. Wait for me there." I hung up. That was bad manners, not saying goodbye. But I needed to get this little rendezvous over with, and I couldn't let my squad have a chance to talk me out of it. I was the leader. I needed to cut the red wire. Or was it the blue wire? Dang it!

"You ready?" Christian asked like he was picking me up for a date.

Right. Ride home, my rear. I felt sick. It felt unnatural to be getting in another boy's car. I just wanted Aiden. I wanted my sweetie.

Instead, I nodded and led the way through the overgrown side yard to the street. Christian jogged ahead of me to the car and opened the door for me to get in.

Well, that was polite. But I wasn't impressed. It only succeeded in making me uneasy. When he closed my door and ran around the front of the car, I closed my eyes. This might not go well. In fact, I might just have to do something I didn't want to do: be rude.

I didn't have to give Christian directions to my house. He already knew where it was. See, total stalker. When he pulled into my driveway, he cut the engine. Pirates of the Caribbean! What did he want now?

He exhaled. "Okay, so I know this may be coming off as a little frightening, but I swear I'm not a creep or anything."

"You sure?" I was angry. I was angry that I'd let myself be so vulnerable to a stranger. I had to tell Aiden. He shouldn't find out from Christian.

"Tessa," Christian said. "I'm not, like, going to blackmail you or anything, if that's what you're worried about."

I turned to him, feeling a little less terrified. I *had* been afraid of that. "What do you want, then?"

He smiled but stared down at his steering wheel. "Well, you already know I like you . . ."

I shifted uncomfortably.

"But more than anything, I just want to help you. You're in over your head. You could have been killed tonight."

He was right on both accounts. "Can't you just drop this?" I pleaded. "Forget that you know?" It was a long shot, but worth asking.

He shook his head. "No. I can't."

So it was blackmail. "And how do you propose you *help* me, Christian?" I felt prickles of anxiety crawl over my skin as I looked over the interior of his car. It was a Honda. Old, but clean. Such a sensible car. And yet I felt trapped. In this situation, I was trapped.

"I just want to spend time with you. And I think I can help with SOS."

That couldn't happen. My eyes glazed over with a sense of dread. "How did you find out about us anyway?" I asked, my voice monotone. I felt completely overtaken.

"I saw some of your notes to Cassandra Heart."

I faced him. "What? She let you see those?" We'd helped Cassie! She knew all communication was top secret. How could she betray us?

"She didn't really mean to tell me," he said, as if he thought it would make me feel better. "It was sort of in the heat of the moment—"

"You hooked up with Cassie?" There was a tug in my chest. It wasn't jealousy or anything, just surprise. Okay, maybe a small bit of jealousy. I thought I was the only one he stalked.

"I was with her once." He shook his head. "Right after she found out about her boyfriend. She went on and on about these pictures, and then I remembered seeing you at Applebee's. So I started following you. Then I spotted you at mini-golf and then later on some guy's porch. I put two and two together, but I haven't said a word to anyone. I swear."

I met his dark eyes, trying to decide whether or not he was telling the truth. He looked honest, but didn't I look honest? And I was a liar. Aiden.

"Aiden doesn't know," I blurted. Suddenly, I felt a tear run down my cheek. Jolly Green Giant! Now I was crying in front of Christian. I was so completely vulnerable.

Christian's mouth opened, but he didn't say anything. I wiped my cheeks quickly, embarrassed by my temporary lack of control. I pulled it together.

I sniffled. "Sorry."

"It's okay. I won't tell him."

That made me feel better. Relieved. "So that's it?" I asked. "You're not going to tell anybody?"

He smiled softly at me. "I won't."

"And you're not asking for anything in return other than quality time."

He paused. My heart stopped. "That's all. Just time with you. Helping you."

"I can take care of myself."

"You fell off a roof."

I rolled my eyes. "You're exaggerating."

Christian shook his head and reached out to touch my knee. My body flinched. Oh, no. I would not stand for this.

"Don't do that," I warned. "I have a very good high kick."

He chuckled, picking a leaf off my pants and holding it up to me. "Relax," he said. "I'm trying to look out for you."

I stared at him, confused. "Why?"

He shrugged. "I don't know. Because I like you. I like how you make me feel. You're just good, Tessa. I don't know how else to explain it. And I think *somebody* should be looking out for you. Your boyfriend isn't doing a bang-up job."

"Don't talk about Aiden like that," I said quickly. But did I disagree? Aiden had been different lately. Distant. I . . . I was lonely.

"Besides," Christian said with a smile. "I'd be good for stuff. Like for when you fall off buildings."

I laughed. Yes. He did try and catch me, and that was chivalrous of him. I exhaled, still watching him carefully. I had no idea how to handle this. My gut was telling me that this was a terrible idea, and my gut was rarely wrong. But then again, I was in a very awkward formation. Not only was my reputation on the line, it was for the other Smitten Kittens too. I had to look out for my girls. I always looked out for them.

"One assignment," I said, holding up my finger. "That's it."

He grinned. "Three."

I stared at him. I didn't have the energy to apply my keen negotiation skills. "Two."

"I can live with two."

Could I? This was not a great thing. I had to tell Aiden. Somehow, I had to tell him before things got even further out of my control.

Christian seemed satisfied and restarted his car, reminding me that I had to go. I still needed to meet the girls at Leona's.

"I'll . . ." What should I say? Thanks for being my trampoline? See you on Tuesday at the movies to spy on Isaac Park? I opted to keep it simple. "Good night." I reached for the handle.

"Tessa," he said. I turned to him. "It was nice hanging out with you."

Fudgsicle! How could he be polite at a time like this? "Uh . . . bye." I got out. There was no need to respond when I wasn't "hanging out" with him by choice. He just showed up to basket-catch me. I didn't fall on purpose.

I paused in my driveway and waited until Christian's car pulled away before I took out the cell phone. Kira needed to know what was going on with our newest addition. But I paused. I put the SOS phone back in my purse and pulled out my cell to dial Aiden.

He answered on the first ring. "Hello." He'd been sleeping. I closed my eyes.

"Hi," I said.

"Tess? What's up, baby?" There was a rustling of sheets.

"Can I come over?" I asked. Tears were stinging my eyes. He would be so angry with me when he found out. I was so scared to tell him. But I had to. Then I wouldn't have to do anything with Christian, and there'd be no more sneaking around. Ever.

"Of course," Aiden said, sounding more alert. "You need me to come get you?"

"No." I opened my eyes and looked at my car, parked off to the side. "I'll come in the window."

"I like when you sneak in my window," he whispered.

My body ached. All I wanted was for SOS to uncomplicate itself. I should've told Aiden from the beginning. I could barely remember now why I hadn't.

"Tess, you okay?"

No. I wasn't. I was very *not* okay. "Yeah. I'll see you in ten minutes."

I closed the phone and paused, thinking back to the night Mary told us her idea for SOS. Everyone had thought it was crazy. But I hadn't. I'd liked it. I wanted couples to stay together, but to stay together honestly. The idea was a slam dunk as far as I was concerned. Because I'd always wondered why my dad had left for so long. I always wondered if it was another woman.

A breeze blew through my hair and I shivered. Our first assignment. I wrapped my arms around myself, thinking of Caleb Perkins. Two years ago, he was Aiden's best friend. He'd also been cheating on his girlfriend.

That was it. That was why I hadn't told Aiden. Wow. I hadn't thought about it in years. When Caleb's girlfriend saw those pictures of him hooking up with another girl, she freaked. She was the senior class homecoming queen, and she proceeded to destroy his rep. In fact, it'd gotten so bad he'd had to transfer schools. Aiden had been distraught.

And yet I'd let him stress over it, never telling him that it was me—that it was me who'd taken the pictures. Now it seemed so stupid for that to be the reason I'd kept the secret for so long, but what could I do now?

I put my palms over my face, trying to gather myself. In this moment, I wished I'd never heard of SOS. Or cheaters. Looking down at my clothing, I realized I was still dressed like a ninja. Aiden couldn't see me like this. I readjusted my pack and turned to go inside my house to change.

I called Kira and set up a meeting before school. I didn't mention Christian. I'd tell them tomorrow. He was my problem, and I'd deal with him. But the squad needed to know that he'd be around.

Over the last two years, not one client that we helped had outed us. It was total girl-code: a survivor's bond. But Christian wasn't obligated by any set of female ethics, or possibly by any ethics at all. I just hoped he could keep a secret; otherwise, the Smitten Kittens would be toast.

My adrenaline carried me up the wooden slats of Aiden's lattice quickly. He'd left the window open, and he sat up when I swung my legs over.

"Hi, baby," he called from the bed, looking all Hugh Hefner in a robe. I quickly wondered what he had underneath it. I was happy his mother's bedroom was on the first floor. I might need more than a foot rub tonight.

I smiled. Just smelling his room, perspiration with a hint of soap, felt so natural to me. So much better than the smell of Christian's cologne, which still lingered in my nose. Stop. I didn't want to think about him. Not here.

"Where were you?" Aiden asked, getting up to meet me at the window, closing it quietly behind me.

"Tonight?"

"Uh . . ." He nodded. "Yeah. I called you like five times."

Shoot. Where had I told Aiden I was going to go? I blanked. Great Scott! This was already going badly.

"Tessa?" he asked.

I met his gorgeous green eyes, and I could see they were so concerned. But he was too adorable to have his brows pulled together like that. I used my thumb to smooth out the wrinkle between them.

"Let's not talk about me," I said, trying to channel my inner perk. "What have you been up to? I missed you."

"Really?" He grinned, leading me toward his bed. He smoothed out the plaid comforter and then patted it. "Sit down," he said. "I made you hot chocolate."

Aw. That was just about the sweetest thing he could have ever done. I saw the World's Best Athlete mug on the side table and grabbed it, taking a sip. My eyes weakened as I looked at him.

"You . . ." I almost cried. "You put marshmallows in it?"

He chuckled. "You sounded down. I wanted to pick you up."

I stared at him as he stood in front of me, his robe tied shut. I closed my eyes.

"Do you remember Mary Rudick?" I asked suddenly. This was it. My heart was beating so fast, I thought I might pass out. I was vaguely aware of the pulsating in my ankle.

"Kyle Turkowitz's ex-girlfriend?"

I nodded. "She was a great captain," I said. My eyes had begun to water. Orion's belt! Please let me be brave enough to tell him.

"She was good," Aiden agreed as he sat down next to me. "Why are you thinking about her? Doesn't she live in California?"

"Yeah." She was lucky. After starting all of this, she was able to have a life now. And she probably had a boyfriend she didn't have to lie to.

We were quiet for a minute, and then Aiden reached out to take my cup, setting it back on the side table. "Come hug me," he whispered. "I want to hold you."

And I couldn't say another thing. I practically collapsed into Aiden's arms, crying softly as he stroked my hair.

"Oh, baby," he murmured. "Is it your parents? Are they splitting up again?"

I sniffled, but I didn't answer. Instead I pulled back, looking

into his beautiful green eyes. All this time, I could have told him.
But now it was too late. He couldn't find out. I'd do what Christian
wanted and soon, I'd be like Mary Rudick. Aiden would be away at
college in a few months and after that, just one more year of SOS.
One more year of lying.

"I love you," I said. "I couldn't even cheer without you in my
life."

He smiled. "Tess." He put his palms on my cheeks and drew
me close to him. "I'll never not be in your life. You *are* my life,
baby."

Aiden kissed me softly, tenderly. Then he laid me down and
tucked me between his flannel sheets as he curled up next to me.
He stroked my hair, murmuring in my ear. Then, to the sound of
his heartbeat, I drifted off.

SOS
CHEATER INCIDENT REPORT

CASE: 054
CLIENT: Emily Hodges
SUBJECT: Wiley Penchant
FINDINGS: At approximately 2 a.m. on March 3, Mr. Penchant was observed leaving the Windmill hotel with a female other than the client. Upon further investigation, it was revealed that the accomplice was Mia Hodges, the client's sister. Mr. Penchant and Ms. Hodges left the hotel in different vehicles, but before leaving, Ms. Hodges was overheard saying, "You can't tell her, Wil. She'll be devastated. I love you too, but Emily can't find out."

Enclosed are the photos documenting the time the two spent in the hotel room. Surveillance captured footage of them kissing, along with other sexual situations. Mr. Penchant also gave Ms. Hodges a box and wished her a happy "one-year anniversary." It was not clear what they were celebrating.

SOS is confirming this cheat, and considering the severity of the findings, we would also like to extend our list of reputable therapists. You will find it enclosed with the photos.

We trust that this report will remain confidential as some of the information contained within could compromise our top-secret status.

SOS is sorry for your loss, and we offer our deepest sympathy. We hope that we will not have to assist you again in the future, but please keep us in mind for referrals.

Keep smiling,

SOS
Text: 555-0101
Exposing Cheaters for Over Two Years

CHAPTER THIRTEEN

"QUEEN OF SHEBA!" KIRA GASPED, DROPPING HER maroon and gray pom-poms on the wood floor. "He knows?" She sat down, stunned.

I nodded. The squad was not taking the news well. Neither was I. I hadn't even ironed my cheer skirt this morning. In fact, my braid had strands of hair dangling from it.

"Is he going to tell?" Leona asked, looking around the empty gymnasium. Poor thing. She was so nervous. She'd actually chewed off three of her fingernails. Her French manicure was ruined.

"Well," I began, pacing in front of the bleachers as they sat watching me. It was hard to look composed when I felt so broken. "He said he wouldn't. But he's asked to help."

"Help?" Kira squeaked with relief. "That's so sweet!" She was beaming.

I tried to smile, but my belly turned. Christian had said he was worried about me, but I knew the score. All I had to do was indulge him in two assignments. It wasn't like I had to hook up with him. Thank heavens he knew better than to ask for that. That would have earned him a swift kick to the groin.

"How did he find out?" Leona asked. I stared at her for a minute, unsure if I should tell. Cassie had messed up, it was true, but it was no reason to subject her to Leona's wrath.

"I don't know," I said. "And it doesn't matter now." But there was something else I wanted to talk to them about. Something I'd realized as I snuck out of Aiden's window in the middle of the night.

"After the Christian situation is resolved . . ." I paused. "I think SOS should take a break."

They all gasped.

"What about the cheaters?" Izzie squealed. "We're just going to let them get away with it? Look at what happened to Emily Hodges—her boyfriend was sleeping with her sister!" Izzie looked sick. We'd caught her boyfriend with her cousin just last month.

"Tessa," Leona spoke up. "Can you imagine the cheater stats if we stopped tracking them? They'd be out of control."

"They're already out of control," Izzie whined.

"Even more reason to keep on it," Leona shot back.

Kira stood up, waving her hands wildly. "Be quiet and let Tessa have the court."

I took a deep breath, glancing from face to face. Their expressions told me one thing. I'd be a quitter. If I didn't stick it out, I'd be a quitter.

"Never mind," I said quietly. "I'm just tired."

"You look it," Leona muttered. I was glad I'd never let her lead a practice. Her attitude was less than sparkly sometimes.

"Tessa," Kira said, turning to me, looking serious. Her usual wide-eyed expression was gone. This was the real Kira, the one that kicked tush. She marched over and hugged me tightly.

"You're choking me," I said.

"Sorry." She backed up and tilted her head. "If you want to stop SOS, I'll follow your lead. After all, we'll still be Smitten Kittens. Even without the spying."

She was a peach. An absolute Georgia peach. "Thanks, K."
Starry night! I was going to cry.

But the bell rang, signaling that we were all late for first period.
I sucked up my sorrow and straightened my posture.

"Shoot," Izzie said, bounding toward the gymnasium door. "I'm
going to get the tardy chair!"

Kira groaned and jogged over to get her pom-poms from the
floor before leaving, and Leona mumbled something to me about
writing a letter to the school board as she walked out. I exhaled,
knowing one positive thing. No matter what, the Smitten Kittens
would always stick together.

I was late for history. The class I shared with Chri—
Fiddlesticks!

Scooting in three minutes late, Kira and I were assigned lunch
detention in front of the entire class. No surprise there. What was
alarming was the fact that Christian was absent, leaving his seat in
the back row empty. It made me pause in my distrust for him. I'd
thought he'd show up to gloat, stalk, or at least gaze, knowing that I
was pretty much at his mercy. But he didn't. I was relieved.

The relief didn't last long, though. Ten minutes later, he walked
into history. His hair was pushed behind his ears, his cheeks rosy
with what looked like athletic exertion. It was . . . attractive. I folded
my hands in my lap and glanced away. My neck felt slightly warm.

"Nice of you to show up, Mr. Ferril," Mr. Powell said. "And I'm
sure you'll be happy to hear that you get to share your afternoon in
lunch detention with two cheerleaders."

Christian chuckled, and when my eyes met his, he winked. My
stomach turned, and my fingers began to tremble. He walked past my
table, and Kira tapped me on the thigh with her purple pom-pom pen.

"Tess," she whispered, her eyebrows pulled together. "Do you think . . . do you think Christian is helping because he's still crushing on you?"

I laughed. I didn't know how else to react. He'd been obvious, and even though I knew it, I'd still let him hang around me. Was it any wonder my life was about to fall apart? Strawberry shortcake! I felt sick. Really si—

"Mr. Powell?" I raised my hand.

"Yes, Ms. Crimson."

"I need the nurse. Now." I stood up, knocking my chair into the table behind me, but before I could make my way to the exit, I leaned over and threw up on the linoleum floor of the classroom. I'd had Froot Loops for breakfast, and it made my puke all rainbowy. It was almost cute, but still, it got on my sneakers. Gross.

Kira was there, moving my braid of hair away from my mouth and rubbing my back. "Oh, Tess!"

My head was swimming. I could hear the class behind me, most of them sounding disgusted; a few laughed. Suddenly, everything just felt so out of control. Tilted.

"Ms. Crimson," Mr. Powell said, moving from his podium to come to stand near me. "Are you okay?" His voice was kind. I appreciated that.

"No," I said, wiping my mouth with the back of my hand.

"Do you want me to have the nurse come get you?"

I shook my head, but it made me dizzy. I put my hand on the cool table to steady myself.

"I'll take her," I heard from behind me. A hand slid around my waist, straightening me up. Christian.

"No," I said, trying to push him back. But I felt weak. "Kira?" I turned to look at her for the first time. She was pure white.

She shook her head. "Let him, Tess," she said apologetically. "You know how much I hate chunky things." It was true. The girl didn't go anywhere near stew or cottage cheese.

Shutterbug! Once again, I was at the mercy of Christian. It was like he had control over every part of my life, including my health.

"Let go of me," I said, wiggling out of his grasp as he tried to touch me again. The classroom door opened, and the janitor came in, sloshing a rolling bucket behind her. I quickly wondered if she had vomit radar but then realized time had passed while I stood, trying to gather myself. Someone had even opened a window.

My stomach turned again. I needed to move.

I quickly stepped forward, careful to avoid my puke, and despite my clear resistance to his help, Christian found a way to get his hands on me again. He held my elbow and led me out of the classroom just as the sound of water splashed on the classroom floor.

The minute we got into the deserted hallway, I stopped. My vision was beginning to clear. I still couldn't understand what had happened. I'd thrown up more in the past few weeks than I had in my whole entire life. It must have been stress-related, and I had a feeling that I knew the source of it.

"What are you doing?" I asked Christian, using my hands to smooth back some of my loose strands of hair.

"Saving you again." He sounded amused. "Obviously." I stared at him for a minute, unsure of whether or not to trust my gut or the things Christian said. He certainly hadn't tried anything, and yet I couldn't help but feel uneasy around him. Actually, the better word was *queasy*.

"Come on," he said, laughing a little. "I'll take you to the nurse, and you can tell me about our first assignment."

"No—"

"You agreed to two," he interrupted. "And you wouldn't go back on your word, would you, Tessa?" He smiled as he said it, like it wasn't a threat.

I glared at him, and the small smirk stayed on his lips. They were nice lips, sort of full. But they weren't mine. The lips that belonged to me were about ten inches higher. I closed my eyes.

"So if I go back on my word . . ." I took a deep breath. "Are you going to tell my boyfriend?"

Christian chuckled. "Come on, Tessa. Hanging out with me can't be *that* bad. Would it really be worth telling Aiden? It's not like I'm going to attack you."

"Well—"

"Not unless you want me to," he added.

A tingle spread over me, and I was suddenly alarmed. Only Aiden was allowed to make me tingle there. I took a step back.

Christian shook his head. "I'm kidding," he said, reaching out to touch my forearm. "Let's take you to the nurse's office. You look pasty."

I felt weak, so I let him pull me along, not saying anything. I didn't want him to touch me. Definitely not. And yet I let him lead me, not fighting back anymore. I wondered if I'd already become his prey.

As soon as Christian left me alone with the nurse, I began to feel better. Her perfume didn't even make me nauseous. I waited for Aiden, knowing that Kira would find him and tell him what had happened. Not that he wouldn't hear about it anyway. I mean, I threw up in history class. That was news.

Second period started. I chewed on the corner of my lip, glancing at the clock. There was an ache in my chest. Why hadn't my sweetie come to check on me? I glanced over at the nurse, who was keeping herself busy refilling the canister of cotton balls.

Aiden. My eyes began to sting, and I lay back down on the cot.

"Are you feeling sick again, Ms. Crimson?" The nurse looked concerned. I was glad someone was.

"Yeah," I said. "Can you call my mom? I think I need to go home."

"Oh, honey," my mother said as she drove. "You look so pale."

I nodded, unable to shake the dread as I rested my head against the cool glass of the passenger window. My life felt so off balance. It was like I was on the top of a human pyramid with an unstable base.

My mother swallowed hard, and I could sense she wanted to talk to me. It was rare that she wasn't humming or talking. This awkward pause was disconcerting.

"Tess?" she asked. "Is everything . . . okay?"

I turned to her, slowly, lifelessly. "Why?" But I could tell by the way she looked at me that I didn't seem well.

She blinked and then turned back to the road as she slowed down for a red light. "I don't know," she said, looking sideways at me. "You seem to be tired all the time, and I haven't really seen Aiden around."

I glanced at my lap, staring at my jeans and wishing I were wearing my uniform. The sight of the gray and maroon colors sometimes cheered me up. "We've been getting together a lot at night," I said quietly. "When you and Daddy are at the club."

My mother gasped. "Oh, no. Is that what this is, Tess? Is it because we've been gone too much?"

I shook my head. She sounded so guilty, poor thing. How could

I tell her it was my own fault that I was down? It was the sneaking and the lying and the boy who was after me. How could I tell her that I was losing Aiden?

"That's not it, Mom," I said. "You guys are strawberry smoothie. It's . . . it's nothing." I was lying again. To my own mother.

"Tessa," she said softly. I turned to her, desperately lonely. "You don't have to be perfect, honey. Everyone gets sad sometimes."

"Not me." And I tried to smile. Because the worry lines on my mother's face were almost too much for me to handle. She had her own life. She shouldn't be concerned over mine. She needed me like this. She needed me to be a Smitten Kitten.

"Really, Mom," I said, straightening my posture. "I'm liquid gold right now. I just felt a little sick. I haven't been eating well." Everything inside me ached, but as I forced the perk, I started to feel it. Soon, I was myself again. Grinning, chatting.

When we got home, I helped my mother reorganize the cabinets after she made me chicken soup. It was nice to stay busy, something to keep my mind off the fact that my phone didn't ring once. Well, the SOS phone vibrated four times, but my phone didn't. Maybe Aiden didn't know. He'd call me after lunch, though. He'd surely find out then.

But lunch came and went. It was really hard to beat my mother at chess when I kept picking up my phone, checking to make sure I hadn't missed a call or accidentally left it on silent mode.

At three my mom had to go pick up my father from the airport. He'd flown down to San Francisco a few days ago, trying to book them a huge gig. I was glad he'd be back. I'd missed our talks.

Three thirty. School had let out close to forty minutes ago. No

Aiden. I made myself a cup of hot tea and debated whether or not to put on my uniform, just for morale.

I had curled my legs under me on the couch and reached out to grab the remote off the coffee table when the phone rang. I nearly dropped my tea as I quickly set it down and snatched up the phone, pressing it to my ear. "Sweetie," I whined. "Where have you been?"

There was a chuckle, and my belly took a swift turn. "Shoot, Tessa," Christian said. "I just saw you a few hours ago."

I closed my eyes. Not again. "You really shouldn't call me," I said, unable to hide the disappointment in my voice. Where the heck was my boyfriend?

"You're right," Christian replied. "Would it be better if I just came by?"

"What?" My heart rate sped up. He'd become so aggressive in his hunt. It was really throwing me off. "No. You can't—"

"I'm kidding." He was laughing. "You need to lighten up."

"Oh, I'm light," I mumbled. "Like a feather." I put my forearm over my eyes and leaned my head back into the couch cushions. I just wanted Christian out of my life.

"Listen," he said, still sounding amused. "Kira caught up with me after school, said you guys were going on assignment tonight. I wanted to check and see if you were still up for it."

Dang it. I wanted to get my two nights with another man over with, but could I really do this? Especially when I seemed to throw up at the drop of a pom-pom these days.

"Fine," I said, surprising myself. Wait. Really?

"Really?" he asked.

"Yeah. Meet me in front of my house at eleven. We're . . . going to the movies." I hung up and dropped the phone on the couch next to me.

Napa Valley! I'd just made a date with another boy. I groaned and collapsed into the cushions, covering my head with my arms. My phone rang again.

Okay, now he was going to get an earful. I sat up, my pulse racing, and brought the receiver to my ear. "What now?" I said, much ruder than I had been in years.

"Tess?" Aiden asked. "Is that you?" He sounded confused. I was horrified.

"Hey," I said. "Sorry, yeah. I . . ." I couldn't tell him I'd thought he was someone else, because who else could it really be other than a Smitten Kitten? And I'd never be rude to them.

I walked to the kitchen table and sat down on a hard wooden chair. I was talking to my sweetie; I should feel relieved. Instead, I felt anxious. Unsure.

"Heard you got sick," Aiden said casually.

"Did you?" A bit of anger prickled down my back. "Were you worried?" I rested my elbow on the linen tablecloth as I put my palm over my forehead.

"Of course, baby." He laughed. I clenched my jaw.

"I could tell," I snapped. Holy crow! I was being sort of mean. Who was I?

"What?" Aiden asked. I heard the phone shift on his ear. "What's wrong with you? Are you pissed at me or something?"

Oh, my word. I could feel the beginnings of a fight. But it wasn't fair! He couldn't just forget about me like that. I would never forget about him.

"You know what?" I said, beginning to choke up. "I am PO'd.

You didn't come to find me. You didn't call. In fact, Aiden, you've been out of school for over an hour, and you're just now getting ahold of me. Where were you?" I didn't sound like myself. I was acting crazy. Paranoid. Suspicious. SOS was getting to me. But Aiden paused, and there was a sickening twist in my belly.

"I was working on a chemistry lab assignment, Tessa."

No. Oh, no. I took the phone away from my ear for a second, breathed out, and then brought it back. "With Chloe?"

"Yeah. We stayed after. I didn't find out you were sick until just now when Kira called."

"Where were you at lunch?" I needed to curl up in a ball and sob. In about ten seconds, I was going to do just that.

"Same thing, baby. Working on chemistry."

Small little aches began to break across my face, wanting me to cry. "So," I said, trying to sound as composed as possible. "You spent the entire day with Chloe?" Sugar and spice! I would die.

"Don't say it like that," Aiden said, sounding annoyed. "Damn, Tessa. Do I say shit when you hang out with that prick?"

I was startled. Aiden knew better than to swear like that. "Stop," I said.

"No."

My eyes widened. What was going on? Things were so clearly upside down. My boyfriend was angry with me when I was the one being ignored. He'd spent the entire day with that little cougar!

"I have to go," he said quickly. "I'm sure you're busy tonight." He was definitely upset. And correct. I was busy.

"Sort of—"

"Whatever. I'll see you tomorrow or something, Tess. Whenever you can fit me in."

And. He. Hung. Up.

The phone fell from my hand, bouncing on the table. Aiden had never, ever hung up on me. Not ever.

My life had just officially fallen apart.

"Hi, Daddy." I walked up to give him a kiss as he came in the door, dragging his suitcase behind him.

"Hey, sweetie." He sounded confused, pulling his brows together. "You do something different with your hair?"

The braid had been hurting my head so I took it out, letting my hair run wild with crimps.

"I came home sick from school," I said, as if that had ever stopped me from looking great before. "Where's Mom?" I peeked over my father's shoulder as he was closing the door.

"She's going to the club. We're staying in town tonight. She . . . she said you were upset with us for being gone so much. Is that true, Tess?"

My mother. She'd obviously been obsessing about our earlier conversation. I was making her unhappy. I was making everyone unhappy.

"That's not it," I said. My father moved his glasses down his nose to look me over slowly. Then he adjusted them and motioned to a kitchen chair.

"Take a seat, kid. Looks like you need to talk."

I smiled. If only I had talked sooner, I wouldn't be in such a mess. I plopped down in the seat and waited as my father poured us both a glass of milk and grabbed a few oatmeal cookies out of the cupboard. He was adorable. I was such a lucky Kitty.

"Thanks," I said, taking a cookie from him as he sat down.

He nodded and then cleared his throat. "All right, Tess. Spill."

I chewed slowly, wondering what my father would think of my spying. Wondering if he could relate more to the cheaters than to me. "I'm in trouble," I said.

His eyes widened. Oh. I guess that wasn't the best thing for a teenage girl to tell her father.

"Not that sort of trouble," I said quickly. He exhaled.

"Wow, Tessa, thanks for the heart attack. Now what exactly have you gotten yourself into?" He pushed back in his seat and crossed his legs, taking a sip from his glass.

"Daddy, do you think Aiden is tired of me?" I hated those words. They were entirely too close to possible.

My father choked on his milk, his face turning red as he leaned forward. When he was able to breathe again, he put his hand on my arm and shook his head. "Has something happened with Aiden?" He was terrified. Aiden was the son he wished he had.

"No, not yet—"

"Not yet?" My father raised his voice. "Are you two having problems? Is it his mother again?"

"No, she's the same. But Dad, do you think . . . maybe Aiden wants to see other girls?" Good golly! I began to tear up.

"What other girls could there be?" he said so seriously, I had to smile. In my father's eyes, I was perfect. Even if it wasn't true, that was what he thought. He reached over to mess up my hair.

"Stop." I laughed, pushing his hand back.

He pressed his lips together, looking at me thoughtfully. "To answer your question," he said quietly. "No. I don't think Aiden would leave you, Tess. I've seen the way he looks at you. It's the same way I used to look at your mother. He adores you."

But his words, although sweet, stung me. "You left Mom," I said, suddenly needing to know why. If he loved her so much, why did he walk away?

My father dropped his head, and I recognized the look. I'd seen it many times in my line of work. Shame. He had cheated. My father had cheated on my mother.

"I made a mistake," he said, meeting my eyes. "I made one mistake, Tess, and I almost lost her." He waited a beat, and I felt a heaviness creep over my chest, aching.

"Why did you do it?"

"I don't know," he said. "I think I was lonely. But I never meant to hurt her, or you. I love you two so much. You're my life."

Aiden had told me that once.

"And I'm glad your mother loved me enough to forgive me." He ran his hands through his thinning black hair. He tried to smile at me. "Aiden's a good boy," my father said. "He loves you. Why can't you trust that?"

I didn't know. I wasn't exactly sure what had changed. It seemed that everywhere I looked, all I saw were cheaters. I took a deep breath and closed my eyes.

I didn't trust Aiden. I couldn't. Because if there was one thing my heart-to-heart with my daddy confirmed, it was that my boyfriend could love me *and* cheat on me.

But I wouldn't let him.

SOS
DONATION ACKNOWLEDGMENT

Dear Mrs. Pugliese,

Thank you very much for your donation. SOS is a nonprofit organization, and your donations go directly to assisting others with their relationship needs by giving us the funding for the latest surveillance equipment.

Helping your daughter out of an unfaithful relationship was a joy in itself, but your money is much appreciated. We share your hope that Lynny will consider dating again in the future, even though she has taken a lifelong oath of celibacy. We understand your desire for grandchildren.

Once again, thank you for your generosity, and we wish you all the happiness in the world. Have a great day.

Keep smiling,

SOS
Text: 555-0101
Exposing Cheaters for Over Two Years

CHAPTER FOURTEEN

"SO THAT'S REALLY WHAT YOU WEAR?" CHRISTIAN asked, grinning as I approached his car. It was nice out tonight. Warm, clear. It was comfortable. The wind blew through my hair, whipping it out behind me as Christian held the door open.

"Well, we are undercover," I said, climbing in the passenger seat. "You should have tried a disguise maybe." Although he did look nice. Light blue sweater, khakis, very sexy cologne. I, on the other hand, was wearing my black turtleneck and leggings, along with a black down vest that I had lined with pockets to hold wiretaps and handheld audio equipment.

Christian laughed and closed my door softly before walking around his Honda. It was odd being in his car again. Almost familiar. Hm. I didn't want any of this to be familiar. No. I wanted it to be decidedly unfamiliar. In fact, I was going to end this little adventure tonight. I would tell Christian that this was it. Over. Finished.

I was going to call his bluff.

The driver's side door opened, and Christian smiled as he got in, glancing over my body as he did so. He may not have thought I noticed, but my peripheral vision had gotten very good. And he was checking out my C cups. Totally inappropriate.

"Well," he said, starting the car. "Even though you're dressed like a bank robber, you're still the cutest thing I've seen all day."

I chewed on the corner of my lip, maybe blushing a little. "Thanks."

I gazed out the window as he pulled onto the tree-lined street, wondering where Aiden was. Wondering if he was thinking about me.

"Oh, by the way," Christian said, snapping his fingers like he'd just remembered something. "I talked to Kira earlier, told her that we had this assignment covered on our own."

I gasped, swinging to face him. "You did what?" He wasn't serious!

He smiled, shaking his head. "It's not like this is a major mission, Tessa. I'm pretty sure we don't need a chaperone. Unless you're worried that you won't be able to keep your hands to yourself."

Candy canes and unicorns! Had he lost his mind? "Pull over," I said. Obviously, he underestimated the damage a size-seven sneaker could inflict.

"Come on." Christian was laughing. "I can't even joke around with you?"

"No. Not on assignment."

He straightened his mouth, trying to be serious. "You're right," he said. "I need to get my game face on. I'll be good. Promise." He crossed his heart.

I watched him for a minute, and he didn't pull the car to the curb. "Okay," I said. "Let's just get this over with."

"Fine."

"Fine."

We were quiet as Christian continued to drive, bringing us toward the movie theater one town over. SOS had intercepted a call that Isaac Park was meeting a girl there tonight for the midnight showing. He thought he was crafty, but he had no idea that SOS had been on to him for days. And his girlfriend was a total sweetheart, too. Poor thing.

The parking lot was nearly deserted as we pulled in. Not many people went to a midnight movie during the week. Not wanting the car to get recognized, I had Christian park toward the back. After he turned it off, I took a minute to go through my backpack, making sure I had my camera with the night vision lens. Christian was smiling as he watched me twist on the cap.

"You couldn't care less about the mission, could you?" I asked, sliding some of the pieces into the inside pockets of my vest. Theaters usually frowned at bringing in backpacks. He laughed. "Do you want the honest answer?"

I turned to him, not sure that I did. The streetlights filtered in, illuminating his face and throwing shadows over his eyes, making him look almost sinister.

"Check the time," I said, feeling uneasiness creep over me. I didn't want to be alone with him anymore. I wanted to hurry, and then go find Aiden.

Christian leaned his head back against the seat, staring at me. "We don't have to go in," he said quietly. He licked his lips, and I could see how hard he was trying to be smooth, suave. But he looked nervous.

My heart raced and I was completely uncomfortable. And yet there was a small part of me that was attracted to him. At least, to the attention from him. I'd been feeling so bad lately, so imperfect. And Christian was looking at me in that way—the way Aiden used to.

Christian's hand moved from his lap and touched my fingers softly as they lay on the seat.

"Don't," I said quickly, moving my hand from under his. "You can't touch me."

He yanked his arm back, straightening up. "I'm sorry. I can't help it sometimes. I find you fascinating."

Was I a science experiment? Did he want to pin me down and dissect me?

I slid the camera into my purse and pushed the door open so hastily that I nearly fell out. I could barely catch my breath as I started speed walking across the parking lot barely able to catch my breath. Christian was immediately behind me.

"You're freaked out, right?" he asked, sounding apologetic.

"No more talking," I said. I didn't care about the assignment anymore. I just wanted to get the pictures and leave.

We got inside the old-fashioned theater, and Christian rushed ahead to the glass-enclosed ticket booth. I let him buy the tickets as I scoped the scene.

"Do you want popcorn or a soda?" he asked as he came over to me, motioning toward the concessions. I curled my lip.

"Christian, this is absolutely not a date."

"Right," he said, smiling. "Forgot."

I stared at him, not sure if I could trust him to stay undercover. We still had to find Isaac. It figured that he'd talked about seeing some horror movie. I hated them. I wasn't easily scared, but I just felt so bad when people got murdered. It was gross.

Christian agreed to be quiet, but I couldn't help but feel like he was mocking me. Like this was all just an excuse to be around me. I mean, I knew it was, but I also thought he wanted to help a little. It was pretty clear now that he didn't.

We found theater eight, and not surprisingly, it was nearly empty. I let the door close, blocking out the harsh light of the hallway, and searched over the backs of heads. I found Isaac. He wasn't really hard to spot. He wore his hair in a faux-hawk, not a huge one, but a short, brushed-up one. It was sort of cool. Very individualistic.

"They're two rows up," I whispered to Christian and glanced at the screen. It was opening with a murder. I sighed. So sad.

Christian nodded and took my arm, leading us to the back row. We got the corner seats, and I reached into my inside pocket. It struck me that this might just be my last SOS assignment. I swallowed hard, feeling a bit nostalgic. But then I thought of Aiden and how much more time I'd have for him. It calmed my nerves a little.

My camera was poised and ready, night scope on. I zoomed in. Isaac was whispering in the girl's ear, looking sweet. It made my stomach turn. He'd been with his girlfriend, Angela, for close to a year. She was an absolute doll: perky and petite.

I used the camera to push in on the accomplice's face. She was pretty enough—blond and busty. My eyes narrowed. She sort of reminded me of Chloe, but I tried to block that thought. The last thing I needed was to think of Chloe as an accomplice in a cheat. Because I knew exactly who she was after.

"Did you want me to move closer?" Christian whispered. He bent his head dangerously close to mine. His spearmint breath was hot on my cheek.

"Yeah," I said, mainly to get some distance between me and his ridiculously attractive cologne. "Take the recorder and get some audio. I need to know what they're talking about."

I reached in my pocket and pulled out the mini-recorder, passing it to Christian. His fingers touched mine as he took it. I met his eyes.

Okay, so we were pretty close to each other's mouths. His smelled like mint, mine, Jolly Ranchers. My breath was caught. He looked like he was about to kiss me. I didn't move away.

He smiled. "Be right back. Get some good photos." Then he winked and ducked down as he got up and crept down the aisle. I watched him, feeling my heart race.

Brooklyn Bridge! Would I have just let him kiss me? No. I . . . wasn't attracted to him. I loved Aiden.

I shook my head and took aim at Isaac. He was a cheater. I'd never be like that. I wasn't like that. Only, I found myself zooming in on Christian's face . . . admiring it. Then, before I could begin any unwanted fantasy, I shut off the camera, got up, and walked out.

It took close to twenty minutes for Christian to meet me outside. He jogged up to the car as I leaned against it. I was chilled from the cooled air but thankful to now have my wits about me.

Christian stopped in front of me, panting. "What the hell, Tessa?" he said.

"Don't say "hell.'"

He stared at me for a minute, then, "Sorry. What in the *h*, *e*, *double hockey sticks* happened to you?" He grinned.

I couldn't help but smile back. I liked the double hockey sticks thing. After an intense second of looking at each other, I exhaled and put my fists on my hips.

"I'm sorry, Christian," I said. "But I can't do this with you. And I'm done with SOS. I quit." Wow. I wasn't sure if I'd ever said the word *quit* in my life.

"You can't," he said. His eyes were wide. He took a step closer to me. He was now entirely *too* close.

"Tell everyone if you want," I said, uncomfortable with his proximity. I didn't care about SOS anymore. I needed to get my life back. Things had gotten too mixed up, and if the school hated me, fine. I couldn't be perfect anymore. It was just too hard.

"Tessa," Christian said softly, tilting his head. "I'm not going to tell anyone. I'm not trying to hurt you."

My face was tingling. "Then what are you trying to do?"

Christian closed his eyes, and when he opened them, he focused on my mouth. "This," he said, reaching out to put his palms on my cheeks, pulling me toward him. He pressed his lips to mine, forcefully, passionately.

And for a second, I stood there, shocked, stunned, guilty. His mouth felt so foreign to me that it was almost like they weren't my lips he was sucking on. It was like an out-of-body experience. At least it was until he tried to put his tongue in my mouth.

"Stop," I said, bringing up my hands to try to push him back. He was resistant at first, still going for it, so I pushed him hard enough to make him stumble. John Deere tractor! He'd just kissed me. He just . . . kissed me! "You've gone batty," I shouted. "You can't—"

"I'm sorry," he apologized. "I couldn't help it, Tess." He licked his lips. Ew. Was he trying to still taste me? My stomach took a violent turn.

"I'm not going to tell Aiden about this," I said, holding up my finger to him. "Because if I did, he would seriously cream you. But don't effing touch me again. Got it?" The adrenaline pumping through my veins was making my entire body shake. And my mouth tasted like spearmint. Leaping lizards! I needed Aiden.

I turned around and yanked open the passenger door with a creak. I'd never kissed anyone other than Aiden. Ever. This had been a huge mistake. A big, ginormous mistake.

Christian ran around the car and got in, looking unsteady, sort of shaky. He should. He'd just assaulted my mouth with his. So what if his lips were pillowy soft? It was still wrong! He didn't even ask.

We were silent as we drove back through the streets of

Washington toward my house. I stared out the window, happy the night was over but worried about its consequences. Surely Christian would out the Smitten Kittens now.

After he'd turned on my street, Christian pulled into my driveway, bumping the curb on the way in. I looked over at him, not sure if he was mad or flustered. He killed the engine and turned to me, his eyes lowered.

"You were completely out of line," I said. I should have slapped him. That's what a real Smitten Kitten would have done.

"I know," he said, his brows pulled together. "I'm really sorry. I promise it'll never happen again."

"It sure as heck won't! Because we'll never be alone together again. Understand?" This was the tone of voice I used when the Smitten Kittens were distracted while I was trying to teach a routine. I sounded very authoritative.

"So you're not going to let me have my second mission?" he asked, sounding like a stubborn child.

Blazing saddles! Was he was serious? "Uh . . . no. You made it clear that it wasn't the missions you were trying to accomplish. It was me."

He tilted his head. "So? Is that wrong? Did you not like it at all?" Christian looked worried, and I appreciated his insecurity about his kiss. It was vulnerable, and I understood that. But it didn't mean he could walk around putting his mouth on mine.

"I have a boyfriend. I do not want or enjoy anyone's lips other than Aiden's."

"Does he follow that same philosophy?"

My heart stopped. "Excuse me?" I glanced toward my darkened house, feeling like that comment deserved a swift walkout and a car door slam, but I couldn't really move.

"You don't think your boyfriend kisses other girls?"

I glared at Christian and held up my hand for him to stop. "Zip your lip, buddy. Aiden doesn't touch anyone but me!" I waited a second, feeling my nostrils flaring. How dare he? How flipping dare he?

Christian's eyes narrowed, but he didn't open his mouth. Shoot, why would he? It wasn't like he was trying to stick his tongue down my throat. He'd already done that. Jerk.

"Stay away from me," I hissed, grabbing my backpack off the floor. I got out of his car and slammed the door as hard as I could. I smiled to myself, proud of my bravery, as I stomped toward my house. Then, just for good measure, I tossed my hair over my shoulder one last time before I went in.

Nobody was home. I noticed how Christian's cologne seemed to be clinging to my clothes. I needed a shower and maybe some mouth rinse. But as I walked toward my bathroom, I grabbed my phone off the side table. No missed calls.

Oh, my. Aiden hadn't called. Not since he'd hung up on me. I glanced at the clock, and it was late. But after my shower, I had one other mission. To make up with my boyfriend.

I paused at Aiden's lattice, looking up at his window. Hm. It was closed. I couldn't call the house, not without waking his mother. But I needed to see him. I needed to be with him.

My sneaker slid into the wood panels as I began to climb, fighting back my urge to cry. I just wanted my sweetie. I wanted to pull it together.

As I reached the top, I steadied myself and grasped the bottom of the window. Locked. I exhaled. I tapped my fingers on the glass. Why did I feel so nervous? Did . . . did I think someone was in there with him? The thought nearly made me lose my balance. Just then, the window slid open, startling me.

I screamed.

"Tessa?" Aiden asked, poking his head out the window and looking around. I was clutching the lattice, adrenaline pumping through me.

"You almost made me fall," I whispered, trying to catch my breath.

Aiden scratched his head, staring at me, confused. Then he held out his hand. "Get in here," he said. "You're going to kill yourself."

The minute my hand fit into his, I felt an immediate sense of relief wash over me. I let him help me inside his room. Once in, I watched as he reached behind me, closing his window. He wasn't wearing a shirt. Kettle corn! The boy was half naked and looking fantastic.

I ran my hand over his stomach as he came to stand in front of me. He smiled softly, but his eyes were squinted, drowsy.

"Let's go to bed," he exhaled, taking my hand from his body and pulling me forward. But the minute he sat on his bed, I nearly jumped on top of him. I was on my knees next to him, covering his mouth with mine, tangling my fingers in his hair when he pulled back, breaking our kiss.

"Tess," he whispered, his eyes still closed. I paused, looking down in his face. I didn't understand.

"What?" I was panting, feeling desperate. Panicked.

"Baby," he said, looking at me before taking me by the hips to sit me on his lap. He wrapped me up in his arms, holding me as he rested his chin on my shoulder. "I'm super-tired. It's like two in the morning."

"So?" When had the time of night ever affected my boyfriend's stamina? Cheese and crackers! What was happening?

He chuckled. "Look, I'm glad you're here. And I'm sorry we fought earlier. I want you to stay, baby. I've missed the shit out of you. . . ." His voice was raspy, sleepy. "But my mom's home." He collapsed back on his bed and then opened his arms for me to join him. I stretched out next to him as he snuggled up behind me, resting his mouth against the back of my neck. "She's going out of town tomorrow," he murmured, tickling my skin and sounding halfway to sleep. "We'll be together then."

I swallowed hard, not just because I had tingles that were going unsatisfied, but because I was relieved. I was happy to be in his bed. I was happy to smell him, clean and natural.

"I love you so much," I said, but I was ready to cry before I finished.

"Mm . . ." he said, brushing his lips against the back of my neck. "Stop talking, baby."

"Tell me you love me first." I needed to hear him say it. "You have to tell me."

Instead, he took me by the shoulder and turned me toward him. "I love you, Tessa," he breathed, putting his mouth over mine like he was proving it. "I love you. I love you," he mumbled into my lips again and again. And every time he said it, I tried to pull him closer.

I knew he must have felt it too. Felt that we were losing each other.

I successfully ignored Christian through history class. He "pssted" me once, but I didn't flinch. Kira was going wild, dying to know the details of the mission. But I told her that Christian waited in the car. I hoped she wouldn't ask him his version of the night.

When I left class, I practically ran to my locker to meet Aiden, but he wasn't there. He never seemed to be there anymore.

"Hey," Christian said from behind me as I stood, feeling lost, at my locker. I exhaled and turned around.

"What?"

He smiled, his cheeks a little red. "Your recorder," he said, holding it out.

Oh. I'd forgotten about that. "Thanks." Okay, that was a little embarrassing. Not all of his interactions with me ended with a kiss.

"There's some good stuff on there," he mumbled. His brown eyes met mine, and I felt that same uneasiness I had the night before. "I'll see you at lunch, Tess." He pressed his lips into a smile and walked past me down the busy hallway.

I stood for a minute, not sure how I felt about it. I mean, I didn't want to see him again, but jeez, at least he was making an effort. Albeit a completely overboard, slightly scary effort. Still, I wished Aiden would try this hard to see me.

Before the tardy bell could ring, I jogged ahead to class and promised to get my attitude right-side up. I'd tell the Smitten Kittens tonight. SOS was over.

I waited at my locker before lunch, watching as the halls slowly emptied. No Aiden. I waited even after the bell rang, hoping he'd come trotting down the hall, all apologetic for not finding me earlier. Instead, he just didn't show. I dropped my head and made my way to the lunchroom.

It was packed as I paused at the door, looking over the room. It smelled like sloppy joes, one of Aiden's favorites. He was there at the table, adorable as always in track pants and a T-shirt. But a sharp pain twisted in my chest as I noticed Chloe. She was sitting in my spot, next to him, with her hair pulled up into a high ponytail. They were laughing.

I watched for a minute as she twisted dangling bits of hair around her finger, leaning into him as she spoke. Aiden wasn't touching her, but did he need to? Did any of the cheaters that SOS tracked do their dirty work in public?

I took a few steadying breaths. Things were so unusual now that I started to wonder if they'd ever get back to normal. Slowly, I walked toward my table.

Kira clapped excitedly when she saw me; her face lost its worry. Chloe glanced over her shoulder but didn't move. Her rear was firmly planted in my seat.

"Hey, baby," Aiden said casually as I walked up. He didn't stand or reach out for me.

I watched him as I rounded the table and took the only available seat, between Christian and Kira. Goose bumps lifted on my arms.

"Here's your lunch," Kira said, sliding a tray to me. "Aiden already ate your sloppy joe. Why are you so late?"

I looked across at Aiden, my face tingling with the start of a cry. "Where were you?" I asked. Out of the corner of my eye, I saw Chloe smile.

"Oh." Aiden pulled his eyebrows together. "I'm sorry, Tess. Mr. Grimes sent me and Chloe to pick up some slides from the office. I texted you."

I blinked rapidly. My phone was on my side table at home. I'd forgotten it. But the thought of them roaming the halls together made my blood boil. Aiden roamed with me. Only me.

I clenched my jaw. "So how's lab been going?" I was sure my

raging, uncharacteristic jealousy was obvious, but no one seemed to notice. In fact, Aiden just smiled at me.

"Good, baby. How's cheer practice going?" There was a prickle up my arms, but I held his stare. He looked so calm, but there was something in his words. Something . . . odd.

Chloe giggled. "Things have been fantastic," she said to me, not sounding at all like herself. That deep, raspy voice was gone. Instead, she sounded perky. Sort of like . . . me. "He's really the best." She beamed at Aiden and touched his arm.

She. Touched. His. Arm.

Aiden shifted in his seat, moving away from her politely, but he continued to watch me, almost curiously. I'd nearly forgotten that Christian was next to me until his leg brushed against mine. It was enough to make me lose my appetite. It reminded me that he'd touched me last night. Aiden's eyes narrowed at me when I shifted uncomfortably.

"Check this out," Chloe said to him, and he broke his gaze from me. They started glancing through a notebook as she giggled. They were next to each other. That was my seat. I didn't want to be catty; I was a Kitten, but I was about five seconds away from scratching her eyes out.

"Tessa," Leona said from down the table. "Are we having practice later? I really need to talk to you about a new cheer." She widened her eyes behind her glasses. *New cheer* was code for a new assignment. Or sometimes it just meant a new cheer. The look on her face told me it was the first one.

"Sure," I said, exhausted. I was going to tell them SOS was over anyway. They would be devastated, but I needed to get my life back.

Leona bit her lip, looking antsy. She never seemed nervous. She was naturally cool and collected, the opposite of Kira. But right now she was freaking out.

"Peachy," she said, and I knew it was bad. Leona never, and I repeat never, ate foods with fuzz on them. Nope. This was a bad one. My stomach dropped.

"You okay, baby?" Aiden asked.

My eyes shot up to his, but before I could answer, Chloe snapped her fingers. "Shit," she said, looking at Aiden. "We'd better go, A. The library's holding those books for us."

A? She called him flipping A?

Aiden stood up and looked down at me, his face unreadable. "I've got to finish this project, Tess. Do you think you could get a ride home?"

I squeaked but didn't actually answer. "I'll take her," Kira spoke up for me. She was always there when I needed her. Besides, I couldn't move; I was too busy trying not to cry.

Aiden stared at me for a second, shifting his gaze between Christian and me. He opened his mouth like he wanted to say something, but he didn't. Instead, he slowly backed away and then followed Chloe as they left the cafeteria.

"Christian, sweetie," Leona said, leaning forward to look at him. He seemed startled. He hadn't said a word the entire time.

"Uh, yeah?"

"Would you mind giving us girls a moment? We have some super-secret cheer stuff to discuss." She winked at him.

Crocodile Dundee! Was Leona lying to him? I could tell she had a secret. And then I wondered if I was the only one not in on it.

"For sure," Christian said toward Leona, standing up and grabbing his tray. "Tessa, I'll—" He stopped and looked around at the table of Smitten Kittens, all staring at him anxiously. "Never mind," he said. "I'll catch up with you later." I didn't answer as he walked away, his Birkenstocks flopping on the cafeteria floor.

I turned to Kira as Leona jumped up and sat in Christian's seat. Both she and Kira took one of my arms. I was flanked by cheerleaders. This could not be good.

"Show it to her, Izzie," Leona said like she was offering up my last meal. Only it wasn't lobster; it was McDonald's.

Leona put her hand protectively on my low back, but I still wasn't sure what they were protecting me from.

Izzie's eyes were glassy as she stood up to lean her body across the lunch table and handed me the SOS phone. I jetted my eyes between all of them.

"What's the big?" I asked in a tight voice. I almost didn't want to look.

Suddenly, Izzie burst into tears, covering her face with her hands. What the eff was going on? I shook my head and held the cell up in front of my face.

It was a text. It was . . . Oh, no.

SOS
SUSPECT CHEATER FORM

SUSPECT: Aiden Wilder
ACCOMPLICE: Chloe Ferril

Dear SOS,

Another one for you to add to your possible cheater roster. Who would've thought, right? Aiden cheating on Tessa? She's head cheerleader! And I totally thought they were in love. Oh, well, I guess you never know. Hope it's not true.

Cassandra
SOS
Text: 555-0101
Exposing Cheaters for Over Two Years

CHAPTER FIFTEEN

THE WORLD SORT OF FELL APART AROUND ME.
There were colors, and not pretty rainbow ones, but dark, shaded ones. The sounds in my ears began to echo. I stood up, knocking my tray onto the floor but not looking down at it. I dropped the SOS phone onto the table and backed away. Kira's voice was faintly there, calling me, but I looked straight ahead.

It . . . wasn't true. Not after two years. Not like this.

"I have to go," I said absently. "I'll call you later." I began walking out of the cafeteria, not quite sure where I was going, but just away. I half expected a Smitten Kitten to come after me, but no one did. They were devastated. Not only had Aiden been the perfect boyfriend, he'd been *my* boyfriend. And hadn't I been perfect?

As I walked the empty halls, I choked when a few whimpers escaped from my throat, but I recovered. I would never cry at school. No way. I only had about five minutes before the bell would ring, flooding the walkways with students. I needed to escape before then.

The big double doors of the school's front entrance loomed ahead, and I didn't even stop at my locker. I'd get home, find my mom and dad, and ask them. They knew Aiden. They knew he'd never—

I skidded to a stop. I had no way home. Gingersnaps!

"Tess?"

Christian was next to me. He was always there. But rather than give him a dirty look or politely tell him to go away, I burst out crying. Hysterical, drama queen sobbing.

His arm reached over my shoulders, and soon we were walking into the sunshine of the parking lot. I didn't argue, not that I could; I was covering my face, unable to control my fit.

"Shh . . ." he said soothingly, and it was soothing. It was almost nice. I put my head on his chest, smelling him, trying to fight back the last few tears.

"Get in." He opened the passenger door of his car, and I did just that. I got in. Again.

I kept my head against the cool window, my face feeling swollen, as he drove toward my house. I saw the trees and houses as we passed but didn't recognize any of it. And I didn't care.

I cleared my throat. "Do you think there's something going on with Aiden and your sister?" My voice was hoarse.

"Where'd you hear that?" Christian asked.

I turned slowly to him, my lips feeling dry and chapped. "SOS just got a possible cheater form. It was about Aiden and . . . your sister." I resisted the urge to call her a harsh name, but it was so close to the tip of my tongue, I was alarmed. I hadn't sworn in years.

"Oh."

I waited, but that was all he said. "Did you know?" I demanded.

"No." He shook his head, adjusting the heater. "To be honest . . ." He looked sideways at me. "I can't believe that anyone would cheat on you."

My mouth opened in surprise. It was a puppy-dog statement, and despite what had just happened, I smiled. If Christian could be this fond of me, surely Aiden still was?

It gave me renewed hope. "I don't think it's true," I said as a new sense of calm fell over me.

"You . . . don't?" He sounded truly surprised.

"No. I won't believe it." My chest filled with possibility. "Aiden loves me. I'm his life."

Christian didn't say anything, but when he pulled up in front of my house, he shut off his car. He tapped his fingers on the steering wheel.

"Thanks for the ride. I'm okay now." I was perky. If I could stay like this, things would be okay.

Christian pulled his eyebrows together. "Tessa," he whispered. "It's none of my business; you've made yourself clear. But I'd hate to see you get screwed over like this."

I winced, feeling slapped by his words.

"Sorry." He shook his head. "Listen, I'll be honest, I do believe it. And I . . . I want to suggest something."

I didn't like how easily he accepted Aiden's unfaithfulness. But then again, he didn't know him like I did. "No, thanks—"

"One more mission," Christian said. "Just one. No one even has to know."

My stomach flipped, and the air seemed to escape from the car. I hadn't considered—I would never consider—spying on Aiden.

I shook my head.

"You're a professional, Tessa. You run a wildly successful nonprofit organization," Christian said, looking down at the steering wheel. "If he wasn't *your* boyfriend, would you be investigating him?"

"I'm not going to stake out Aiden," I said simply. It wasn't right. It would mean I thought he was cheating, and I didn't. I wouldn't.

"I'll help you," he said softly. "And I promise I am only there to help. No touching you. Nothing."

Right. I may have been upset, but I wasn't stupid. "Not going to happen," I said. He turned to me suddenly.

"Okay, I didn't want to say anything," he blurted, like he'd been holding in a secret for a while. "Aiden's going out with my sister tonight."

My insides collapsed. "What?" No. No. No.

"Man, Tessa," Christian whined. "I hate having to be the one to tell you this." He shook his head. "I never believe Chloe. But she said that tonight they're going out to dinner and then to his house. She told me his mother's out of town."

I gagged but quickly got his door open to dry-heave outside. No puke. My head spun and I dragged myself out of the car to sit at the curb, putting my elbows on my knees and holding my head in my hands. Aiden's mother was out of town. That was true.

Christian got out and walked around the car, his sandals scraping on the pavement. He sat next to me on the curb and then bumped his knee against mine. "I'm sorry," he whispered. "I was trying to not hurt you. You could just dump him, Tessa. You don't have to spy on him."

But a force rippled through me, making me shiver, and then it passed. It was gone. The pain was gone. I had become SOS. I had become the client *and* the spy.

"Where were they going to dinner?" I asked, my voice thick. I felt suddenly cold. Emotionally and physically. I was shaking.

"I don't know," Christian said. He was trying to talk quietly, be comforting. But there was little he could do for me now. I needed to know. I needed to know that it wasn't true.

I turned to Christian and our faces were close, but I didn't feel any tingles. There were no prickles. I was numb. "Pick me up at nine," I said.

Without another glance, I stood up, crossing my arms over my chest, and walked inside my house.

What to tell the Smitten Kittens? They'd want to know what I was going to do about Aiden. I sat on my couch, my sneakered feet on the coffee table as I tried to think of an answer.

I looked at my phone. It didn't ring. I bit my lip, hard enough to make it hurt. Then I marched into my room, snatched my cheerleading uniform, and slid it on before grabbing my car keys and heading back to school.

The squad was waiting for me in the gym, sitting on the bleachers looking downright nauseous. I was glad they were worried about me, but it would make what I was about to say that much harder.

"Tess?" Kira asked, jumping up. Her shoes squeaked as she crossed the floor. She was looking over my uniform, seemingly worried. Most of the girls were in their spandex or workout clothes. I was in complete uniform, ponytail, and ribbons. It helped me feel better. I felt stronger like this.

I waved Kira off and she stopped dead in front of me. Normally, I would have smiled. Instead, I closed my eyes. "I quit SOS," I said quietly.

"No!" Izzie yelled, her shout echoing through the gymnasium as she began to cry.

"Chill out, Iz," Leona said. I looked at her. She nodded at me.

"I'm sorry, girls. I just . . . can't do it anymore. Every day, every boy, all I think is, 'Is he cheating?' Then the one person I should have been sure about . . ." I didn't finish the sentence. I still didn't want to believe it was true about Aiden. The warning signs had all been there. I just chose to ignore them. There was only one more thing to do, and then I was done with the spying business. Forever.

"It'll be okay," Kira said to me, her blue eyes filled with tears. "Maybe—"

"I just quit," I said again, feeling the impact of my words. "It's over. I can't take the lying, the cheating, the broken hearts. . . ." I sniffled. Corn bread muffin! I was going to cry too.

Instead, I cleared my throat. "I can't cheer this weekend." I stepped up to Kira, putting my hands on the shoulders of her spandex top, staring seriously into her face. "K, you're lead until I get back."

She gasped. Leona growled.

The worry left Kira's face, and she jumped up and down, clapping. It sort of warmed my heart. But only for a second, because I knew I was lying. SOS might be over, but there was one more mission. Without the squad. I dropped my head, backing away.

"I'll see you later," I said quietly, moving toward the double doors.

"Tessa," Leona called out. I turned back to look at her. "Be careful," she said.

We stared at each other. Then I smiled like a true Smitten Kitten and left to spy on my sweetie. Or at least, the boy that used to be my sweetie.

Christian's eyes widened as I got in his car, still in uniform. He had gone to the trouble of putting on a fitted black sweater and black pants. There was even a beanie on his console.

"You're . . . you're spying in that?" he asked, sounding unsure.

"Yep. I draw my strength from the skirt."

He laughed, but when I didn't, he turned back to the street. Had I cracked? Possibly. But it didn't matter. After this, everything I ever was could be wrecked. What difference would it make if I were wearing a cheerleading uniform?

"Do you have gear to set up?" Christian asked as he pulled his Honda into the street.

"Don't need it." Wow. I sounded pretty tough—like, monotone tough. Christian looked a little scared, but I was anxious. Numb, yet anxious.

"Tess—"

"I'm not recording anything," I said. "This isn't an assignment. I just need to know, okay? For myself." My eyes stung, and when I looked at him, he met my gaze, looking sorry. It was nice of him to feel so bad for me. He looked guilty, even.

I turned toward the passenger window, feeling dread slowly creep in as I stared out over the darkened streets. Aiden and Chloe. Let it not be true. By Cleopatra's crown! Let it be a lie.

Rolling down the window, I put my face out into the wind. I could remember Aiden at the recycling speech when I was a freshman. He presented the reasons I should go out with him. And his number one was, "Because she lights up my life with her own brand of sunshine." It was even listed on the flowchart behind him.

Then he hopped down off the stage and walked across the auditorium straight to me. I just about died. People were calling out, cheering, laughing.

But rather than saying anything, Aiden just dropped down in the seat next to me and stared straight ahead, as if it was the most normal place for him to be. Stunned, I looked at the side of his face, deciding that it was not only adorable but sweet, too.

I'd turned to the stage and nestled back in my seat, shoulder to shoulder with Aiden Wilder. The rest of the school stopped watching us and looked up at Principal Pelli, who was still standing there, sort of shocked.

Aiden leaned his head sideways toward me, still staring forward. "Is that a yes?" he'd whispered.

I bit on my lip, glancing down as he held his hand out to me. Well, if that wasn't strawberry smoothie, then I didn't know what was. I took his hand—of course I did. And since then, I hadn't let go. So why did he? Why did Aiden let me go?

I sniffled.

"Tessa?" Christian asked. "We'll just wait at his house, okay? We don't need to go driving all over town or anything." He put his hand tentatively on my knee.

I was too sick at heart to push it away. Aiden out to dinner with another girl. I wondered if he'd ever done it before. Put food in his mouth alone with another girl.

I wanted him back. I wanted my Aiden back. My bottom lip quivered and I bit on it, trying to keep it steady.

After a long minute, Christian took his fingers off my body and put them back where they belonged. On the steering wheel. He parked down the street from Aiden's house and cut the engine.

"I brought a couple of sodas, if you're thirsty," Christian whispered, turning the ignition key so that he could put on the radio. He might have been trying to be romantic since he had Radiohead playing low, filtering in through the speakers. I was sure the skirt didn't help keep things platonic. Boys just didn't respect it. It made them all goofy. Just then, Christian glanced at my legs.

Even though I wasn't thirsty, I nodded when he offered me a soda from a cooler in the backseat. We sat quietly, listening to music. It was nearly ten o'clock. Could they still be at dinner?

"So what else did your sister tell you?" I asked. If she was sneaking around with my boyfriend, she'd have something to say about it. The boy was talented at more than just basketball.

"Nothing. My sister hardly talks to me at home. And she especially doesn't talk to me about the guys she's dating."

Hold on. "She is not *dating* Aiden," I said forcefully. I nearly spilled my can of pop. If he cheated, that was one severely messed-up thing, but dating? No. Not likely.

Christian shook his head. "Sorry. You're right. I just mean, she hasn't said anything about him to me. Other than that they were going to dinner."

Franks and beans! I wanted to cry again. I couldn't take this emotional roller coaster I was on. This was all too much. I should just call Aiden and ask him what was going on. He'd tell me. Aiden wouldn't cheat. He would never . . .

His car drove past us and turned into the driveway. I swallowed hard and set my drink in the center console as I leaned forward. My heart rate was through the roof. I couldn't tell if anyone was with him.

Aiden sat in his car for a long time. His outline was visible through the back window. What was he doing? Was she with him? Good golly! I was going to have a heart attack.

His door opened. I held my breath as I watched his long body climb out. He looked nervous, darting his eyes around the neighborhood. I almost didn't recognize him. He was still in his track pants, but he had a baseball hat on, pulled low. A disguise?

"Is Chloe with him?" Christian asked. He was staring at me and not out the window.

"I don't know yet."

I put my hands on the dashboard and tried to steady myself. I was shaking so badly with adrenaline, I felt like I could lift a car or do some other superhuman thing like that.

Aiden turned back to his Jetta and walked around to the passenger door. I gasped. She was with him, wasn't she? I whimpered.

He opened the door. Aiden reached his hand in, and Chloe took it as he pulled her out. She stood up, clad in a cute, yellow sundress, and immediately wrapped her arms around his waist, leaning into him. I moaned.

"There it is," Christian whispered.

No. Not Aiden. Not him.

I began to cry but didn't look away. I felt Christian's fingers touch my knee, and they were warm. He shouldn't have been touching me, but I was too sick to care. My heart hurt.

I stared out the windshield, mumbling to myself, wanting to curl up into a ball. Aiden was looking down at Chloe, his hands at her shoulders, near the thin straps of her dress, while they talked. I wished I had audio. She was all over him, and at least Aiden had the sense to not do anything in his driveway. At least he had that much respect for us.

Then he put his arm around her waist and moved her away from the car so that he could shut the door. What was he doing?

"So sorry," Christian said next to me, squeezing my knee and moving his hand to rub at the skin just above it. I looked over at him. He turned quickly to me and apologized again. I would have thought his concern for me was sweet if I weren't having a complete breakdown. I couldn't even feel his touch.

I focused back in on Aiden. He led Chloe up the stairs to his big front porch as she clutched onto him, his T-shirt balled in her fist. I hated her. I'd never hated anyone in my whole life, but at this moment, I hated her. And if I talked to her, I'd tell her as much.

Aiden turned back, looking over the street guiltily. One hundred percent. One hundred percent of the time, they cheated. I thought that maybe Aiden could be the one exception, but it sure as heck didn't look that way.

As Aiden walked into his darkly lit house with Chloe and shut the door, I covered my mouth with my hands. He'd brought her inside! He was cheating on me. I was too stunned to move.

I was Mary Rudick. I was just like her when she found out about Kyle. I'd become her. I'd become the meaning behind SOS.

"Tessa?" Christian asked softly, his hand moving dangerously close to the hem of my skirt. But I didn't tell him to move it. I didn't care. And I wasn't going to answer him either. Instead, I just stared at Aiden's house, hoping he'd come marching outside and walk over to this car and yank me out. He would tell me he loved me and that this was all a big mistake. That nothing happened or was even going to happen.

The light in his upstairs bedroom flicked on, and my heart officially broke.

No.

No.

Not my Aiden. Not him.

I bent over, sobbing violently. This wasn't real. It was some nightmare, and I was still in Aiden's room, letting him hold me like he did last night. He wouldn't hurt me. Never.

Christian's hand moved off my leg and touched my shoulder. He wasn't Aiden, but I wished he were. I let Christian pull me into him, and I cried against his shirt. Hard.

I'd lost everything. I reached up and wrapped my hands behind Christian's neck as I continued to shake. What would I do? What could I possibly do now?

"Don't cry, Tessa," Christian whispered into my hair. His voice was soft. I liked it.

"I don't understand," I choked out, letting go of him to wipe my face. Christian was holding me tightly, and although I knew I needed to pull away from him, I didn't. I felt so lonely. So dead.

"He's an asshole," Christian said.

"No," I mumbled, trying to let the numbness take me over. I didn't want to cry anymore. I didn't want to hurt.

Christian slid his hand from my shoulder to hold the back of my neck. It was actually very comforting. I suddenly felt protected.

"Shh . . ." he said into my hair. His breath was warm on my ear.

It made me feel special, the way he wanted me. I didn't love him. He wasn't Aiden. But Christian liked me even without the pep. I sniffled and looked at him.

"I want to go home," I said, and slowly began to pull away. Only, when I moved back, Christian kept his hand on my neck, tilting my mouth toward his.

His face was slightly blurry as I tried to look back at it, blinking through my tears.

"You said no touching," I whispered.

"I'll take care of you."

I closed my eyes and shook my head. While his one hand was on my neck, Christian's other touched my leg again. I looked at him, ready to tell him to stop, when he leaned forward, pressing his mouth against mine. He held me to him as his tongue slid into my mouth.

He wasn't mine. And although I wanted to stop, I found myself kissing him back, letting his tongue touch mine. My body was responding despite myself as his hand moved from behind my neck to my shoulder.

He was making out with me, and I was letting him. Why the flip was I letting him?

"I've wanted you since that first day in class," he murmured in between my lips. His hand moved up my leg, but the minute I felt it touch me, touch me in the place where only Aiden had been, I pushed him back, breaking our connection. Wait. What was happening?

Oh. Heck, no! My mind cleared, and I moved to my side of the car and stared at him, pressing myself to the door. My face was on fire, and my breath was coming out in gasps. There was a tingling between my legs, but it wasn't because I was hot for him. I felt . . . violated.

My eyes were wide as I watched him lick his lips. Bloody Mary! He'd just totally taken advantage of my distress, and he didn't care. He didn't care about me. Only one guy did, and I needed him. I needed Aiden!

Desperately, I grasped the handle of the car door and pushed it open, dashing out. Christian called my name in a loud whisper from the driver's window, but I was a cheerleader. I knew how to hustle.

I ran across the street and hopped the curb, headed straight for Aiden's house. I didn't care if Chloe was in there. I didn't even care if she was naked. She was leaving. Aiden was mine. He was my Wildcat.

There was the sound of a car door, and I had the feeling that Christian was coming after me. Chances were that Aiden's front door was locked, so I turned and ran to the side of his house. I got to the lattice and began climbing like mad. My breathing was so heavy, I knew I wouldn't be able to talk when I saw him. And I knew that I'd be in for something awful when I found them together. But I didn't care. I needed him. My mother forgave my father, and I could forgive Aiden. He was my only guy.

"Tessa," Christian whispered up at me as I reached Aiden's window.

I ignored him and put my hands on the cold glass, sliding open the pane. The lattice wouldn't support Christian's weight, so I knew he couldn't reach me. Trying to steady my breath, I threw my legs inside Aiden's window, letting the familiar smell of it fall over me. Then I braced myself for what I'd find.

It was Chloe. Alone and lying across his bed. Dressed. She sat up in shock and stared at me.

"What the fuck are you doing here?" she hissed, looking toward the closed door.

I curled my lip. Not only was she in my boyfriend's room, she was cussing at me. I snapped.

It took me about one and half seconds to reach her before I grabbed her pale-white arm, yanking her off the bed. Her blond hair whipped around, smacking me in the face as I tossed her to the floor. She glared up at me, her yellow sundress pooled around her hips, displaying her white lace panties. I clenched my jaw. She didn't belong in here. I wouldn't let her take my boyfriend.

Chloe jumped up and stepped to me, pushing me hard and making me stumble back a few feet. As I recovered, she wound up and slapped me hard across the face. Ouch. It stung. I'd never been slapped before.

"Snake," I snarled, reaching out to knot her hair in my fist.

"Bitch," she screamed, and she elbowed me hard on the chin. I reached up to put my hand over my face, feeling the vibration through my jaw. But the minute I raised my arm, she punched me hard in the stomach. Shoot. She was kicking my tail.

"You!" I yelled, working through the pain and getting a fresh grip on her hair. "Are a seriously bad person and I hate you!" I swung her around, but she kicked me in the shin so hard, I let her go and fell back on the bed. She lunged on top of me.

"He's mine now," Chloe spat, putting her hands around my neck to choke me. "He knows you're with Christian."

"What?" I tried to say, but, well, she was choking me. Her little revelation gave me a temporary adrenaline rush. I rolled over, taking her with me, and we tumbled off the bed and onto the carpeted floor.

I straddled her and tried to pin her arms down. "I am *not* with Christian," I said in her face. She sneered.

"That's not what my brother will tell him."

My stomach turned, not liking the ominous tone of her voice, but before I could question her further, she punched me in the jaw, knocking me off of her. I was on my back and she got up, looming above me. I scrambled to my feet and put my hands up defensively as she tried to punch me again.

Aiden's door flew open. "What the hell?" he said, looking around.

Chloe used the temporary distraction. The lunatic reached out to pick up Aiden's alarm clock, yanked it from the wall, and threw it at my head. It blasted me in the forehead and for a second, I saw stars. Lots of them.

"Are you nuts?" Aiden yelled at her. I opened my eyes to see him take her by the arm and push her toward his door. "I thought you were too drunk to go home, but instead you're assaulting my girlfriend?"

Girlfriend? I blinked quickly. My head was hurting. "Aiden?" I called.

He turned around and his mouth dropped. "Oh, baby," he said, letting go of Chloe and moving toward me. "You're bleeding, Tess." He put his palm on my face and looked down at me. He brushed my hair away from my head and I felt relief sweep over me; I also felt wetness run down my cheek. But he was looking at me the way he always had. He loved me. He still loved me.

"What happened?" he asked quietly, glancing with concern between my forehead—which was already swelling, from the feel of it—and my eyes. "Why are you here?"

Chloe laughed. Aiden and I both looked at her. Blue light special! I might have a concussion. Chloe swiped the corner of her mouth with the back of her hand, checking to see if it was bleeding. It wasn't, but I wished it were.

Her voice cut through me. "She's spying on you, Aiden," Chloe said. "Your sweet little Tessa doesn't trust you. Why should she? *She* obviously can't be trusted."

Aiden shook his head and turned back to me, grabbing a T-shirt off his desk to hold it to my head. I was bleeding. That wasn't good. But Aiden was taking care of me. I smiled, putting my arms around his waist.

"I'm sorry," I said to him, gazing up into his green eyes. I felt unsteady, out of sorts. "I love you," I whispered to him. "And I don't care what you were doing. I just need you, Aiden. I forgive you." I wasn't sure if my speech was slurred because Aiden was staring down at me, looking completely confused.

"What I was doing?"

Chloe laughed again, but neither of us turned to her.

"Tess," Aiden said. "Chloe called me saying she was stranded at a party and that she needed a ride home. So I picked her up, but she said she was too drunk to go home and that her dad would freak. I told her she could come back here until she felt better." He stepped back from me and then took my hand to put it on the T-shirt that was against my forehead. He dropped his arm. "Were . . . *were* you spying on me?"

If only I weren't so dizzy, I could explain. But I'd just gotten my tush thoroughly kicked by a nasty little blonde.

"I'm sorry," I said, reaching out for him. "Christian said—"

"Christian? What the fuck does he have to do with this?"

I didn't scold Aiden about his language. I'd like to know what the eff Christian had to do with this too. And his sister.

"She was with him tonight," Chloe announced, sounding like a spoiled five-year-old.

Why was she still here?

"Go home," Aiden said to her, without looking back. He was studying my face. And he was being rude to her. I liked it.

"But she was with him, A. Right outside in his car—"

Aiden closed his eyes. "Chloe," he said in a very controlled voice. "Please get out of my house before I call your father to have him come pick you up."

Then it occurred to me. I'd been played. Christian and Chloe must have set Aiden up and I took the bait. I'd . . . let Christian's tongue in my mouth. I swooned.

Aiden reached out to steady me, completely concerned. He removed the T-shirt and examined my head while he chewed on his lip. I should have trusted him. Nothing was 100 percent. Not even cheating.

Chloe huffed and turned, slamming Aiden's door on her way out, making a framed picture of us drop off the wall. She was such a disturbed girl. I hoped she sought help. Possibly in another state.

"Does this hurt?" Aiden asked softly, touching my cut.

"No," I whispered. I could tell he was angry, but I felt better than I had in weeks. There was never a date. It had all been a lie, a plotted-out, evil lie.

"You might need a stitch," Aiden said, finally meeting my eyes. Yeah. He was definitely mad.

"I'm sorry," I said again. I wanted to forget it all. Christian, Chloe, spying. I just wanted Aiden.

He clenched his jaw. "Exactly what part are you sorry for, Tess? Spying on me? Believing I'd cheat on you? Hanging out with that asshole?"

"Aiden."

He moved back from me. "Don't." He tossed the bloody T-shirt on his desk and then pointed at me. "Don't tell me not to swear. I'm going to beat his ass." He stalked to the window, looking out into the night. "Did he bring you here?"

I could tell by the way Aiden was searching the street that Christian's car was probably gone. I wondered if he brought his sister home or if she'd walked. I hoped she walked. She could use some of the exercise endorphins.

"He told me you went to dinner with Chloe and—"

"I didn't go to any goddamn dinner. And why were you with him in the first place?" Aiden demanded.

This was not the time to tell him the truth about SOS. Not when he was looking so unkindly at me.

"I don't know," I answered instead. "But we came here and I

saw Chloe hugging you. And I saw you bring her inside and then the light in your bedroom—"

"You thought I was sleeping with her? I'm . . ." He paused to clench his jaw. "I'm *not* my father. I would never do anything like that, Tessa."

"Aiden—"

"How did you even know she called me anyway?"

"Her brother," I said quietly.

Aiden shook his head, glaring at me. "So you're just sitting in front of my house with another guy, looking in my window? Are you Nancy Drew?"

"No, but—"

"Do you and your little friend spy on people a lot, Tessa? Is that where you've been?"

"Where I've been?" I was confused.

He scoffed. "Yeah. You know—the late nights, not answering your phone. The weird looks back and forth with the squad. Have you been . . ." He paused and took a harsh breath. "Have you been cheating on me, baby?" His face was absolute pain.

"No," I said emphatically. "Of course not. It's just that everything has been so different lately, and I was sad. Then I heard some things about you and Chloe and I just lost it. We showed up here, and then when she went in your house, I started freaking out. I was ready to go home, but then Christian grabbed me and started kissing me, but—"

"Hold up," Aiden said, his eyes narrowed to slits. I froze. This was bad. This was really bad.

I needed to backtrack. "I know, but—"

"He put his hands on you?" Aiden asked calmly. He shouldn't be calm. That was odd.

"Yeah," I said, trying to match his subdued tone. "His hands, his lips, his tongue—"

"You let him put his tongue in your mouth?" Aiden was so pale. I walked toward him, but he put his hands up and crossed the room to get away from me. My stomach turned.

"Did you kiss him back, Tessa? Did you fucking kiss him?" And Aiden's voice cracked as he stared at me, looking devastated.

Great Scott! One hundred percent. It was true, only Aiden wasn't the one that needed to be investigated; it was me. I *had* kissed Christian back, no matter how misguided it was; my tongue was in his mouth too. I wanted to wash it out.

"I did kiss him, but—"

"Tessa," Aiden yelled, looking at me. "Why would you do that?" He put both of his hands on his head. "What the hell? Why would you let him do that? Oh my God!"

He searched the room with his eyes, then turned his back on me, resting his hands against the wall and leaning into it. He dropped his head as small whimpers escaped from him. My entire body ached, and not just from where Chloe had hit me. Aiden was crying, his shoulders shaking violently. And it was my fault.

"Aiden," I called softly.

"What have you done?" he whispered without picking up his head. "Don't you love me?"

Good gravy! Of course I loved him. I walked up and hugged him from behind, resting my face on his back. "I do love you, Aiden. So much. And I was devastated when SOS got the message about you and Chloe—"

"SOS?" he asked, and sniffled. He straightened up and turned in my arms before taking me by the shoulders to move me back from him. "What's SOS?"

Dang it. This was not the time to tell him, but I couldn't lie anymore. Not after all of this. "It's sort of a long story."

His jaw clenched. "As long as the one about you kissing another guy?"

Was there a way back from this? Would Aiden ever forgive me?

"What is SOS?" he asked again slowly.

I swallowed hard. "The Society of Smitten Kittens."

He waited and then adjusted his stance, letting me know that he was getting impatient.

Time to talk. "We investigate cheaters."

"Investigate?"

I couldn't tell if he believed me or not. I bit on the inside of my cheek, meeting his irritated gaze. "You remember the other night, when I asked you about Mary?"

"Yeah."

"Well, after Kyle cheated on her, she started up a sort of club. When a girl thinks her boyfriend is cheating, she'll text us. We . . . sneak around and find out for them."

Aiden licked his bottom lip, staring at me. "If anyone else was telling me this, I'd say they were full of it. But it's you. And I don't know what you've gotten yourself into, but I don't like it. You spy on people?" He sounded disappointed.

I ducked my head. "Yeah."

"Then what?"

"We tell the girls, Leona gives them a cheater incident report, and we let them decide what to do."

Aiden shook his head. It was a lot to take in. I could understand that. "And . . . you've been doing this to me?"

"No," I said, reaching for him again. He let me put my hands around his waist, but he made no move to touch me. "It was just tonight. Someone texted me and said that you were seeing Chloe. I—"

"And it never occurred to you that it could be that asshole? Or his sister? Or just someone messing with you? You just believed it. Wow, Tessa. Wow." Aiden looked up at his ceiling, blinking away tears. I put my head on his chest, wishing he would just wrap his arms around me like he used to.

"I didn't want to believe it," I whispered. "Things between us had just been so different lately. I thought—"

"Because of you," Aiden said loudly. "You're always busy, Tessa. Distant. I didn't know what was going on. I was trying to give you space, but I didn't think you'd hook up with another guy."

I closed my eyes. I had thoroughly effed up.

"And this SOS bullshit. I can't even begin to understand the number of ways it's wrong. My God. Did you break into people's houses?"

"Occasionally."

"How long have you been doing this?"

Uh-oh. "Two years."

His body stiffened. "Two years? You've . . . you've been sneaking around for two years? Our entire relationship?" His voice was controlled, but I knew he wanted to yell. His body had begun to shake. I, on the other hand, was on the verge of getting sick. My head was seriously wounded.

"Yeah," I mumbled. I wanted this to be over. I wanted the healing to begin. Starting with my forehead.

Aiden gasped. "Wait. Did you have something to do with Caleb and his girlfriend breaking up?"

I didn't move. Yes, I did have something to do with it, but I mean, he *was* cheating on his girlfriend. He wasn't an innocent victim or anything.

"Answer me," Aiden said, and he took me by the upper arms and moved my body off of his. He didn't want me touching him.

I nodded. His face was a mixture of pain and anger, and he brought his hands to his face and rubbed roughly at it.

"Who are you?" he asked. He looked at me, sad, confused. "Who the fuck are you?"

His voice was quiet, hurt. Heartbroken. But I was here now. We'd be okay.

"I love you," I murmured. There was a new aching in my chest. A different one than I'd felt earlier. This one was worse because it was my own fault. I'd made this mess. Me.

Aiden's eyes softened a little as he looked down at me. He reached his hand out to run his fingers down my cheek, so gently that I nearly cried. But then he brought his thumb and traced it over my lips, slowly. He swallowed hard.

"You let him touch you here," he whispered. "And now . . ." His thumb paused in the middle of my lip. "I can never kiss you again."

Dropped. My stomach dropped as his eyes glassed over, and then he moved his hand and broke from me. He walked across his room, and I tried to breathe. I wasn't sure I could. I heard his bedroom door creak open.

"Go home, Tessa," he said to my back.

I couldn't turn. Please. Let this not be real. Let me wake up. Please.

"Tessa?" And he was pleading. He wanted me to go. This was the warning before he became rude.

Blinking quickly, I turned to look at him. He stared past me, looking at the wall above my head. He wasn't going to forgive me.

I walked to the door, pausing in front of him, looking up and waiting for him to see me. Finally, his green eyes flicked to mine. They were sad. So very, very sad.

"Goodbye, baby," he said, letting his voice crack.

My lip quivered and I wanted to grab him. But he put his hand on my back and pushed me gently through the door. He walked me downstairs and left me on his front porch. Aiden didn't even look at me again before he shut the door, locked it, and left me outside. Alone.

SOS
DISCIPLINARY ACTION

FROM: Leona
TO: Kira

You have violated one or more of the SOS rules and are therefore subject to disciplinary action. You are hereby suspended for one mission for violating the rule(s) marked below:

- Confirming a cheat with insufficient evidence
- Violating the gag rule
- Reinvestigating a subject (double jeopardy)
- Making personal calls during a mission
- Intervening with a cheat in progress
- Spying on a non-subject

Other:
- X   *Hooking up with the subject of investigation!*
- X   *Wearing heels while on a mission*

SOS
Text: 555-0101
Exposing Cheaters for Over Two Years

CHAPTER SIXTEEN

KIRA TOOK ME TO THE EMERGENCY ROOM AFTER
Aiden called her to come pick me up. It was sweet of him to make
sure I got home okay, even though he wasn't willing to do it himself.
At one point while I was walking, I thought I'd heard someone
following me, but when I turned, no one was there. I chalked it up
to head wound delusions.

Kira had picked me up about a block away from Aiden's house
and driven directly to Good Samaritan Hospital. When we got
there, the blue plaster walls were filled to the brim with patients.
But the nurses quickly evaluated me. Probably because I was still
in uniform.

I needed a stitch, but luckily, I didn't have a concussion. And
although I asked, there was no medication for a broken heart.

As Kira and I waited in the lobby for me to be called back, the
nurse gave me a gauze pad that I held to my forehead. My life was
shattered, and my brain was throbbing. Things would never be okay.

"I'm not trying to be nosy," Kira said from the hard plastic chair
next to me. "But what exactly happened when you and Christian
were in his car?"

I didn't want to tell her. I'd glossed over the details the first time
for a reason. No, all I wanted right now was to listen to coughing
patients and the hum of the monitors.

"I'm a horrible person, K," I mumbled, staring at the receptionist behind the desk. She had on those chic, beehive-frame glasses with a dainty silver chain dangling from them, looped around her neck. I'd have to tell Leona about them. They were fabulous.

Kira gasped. "No, you're not, Tess. You're the greatest person I know."

I scoffed. "I kissed Christian," I said, turning to stare at her. "I was upset and I cheated on Aiden. What kind of person does that make me?"

My best friend smiled and reached out to take the gauze from my head, checking my wound. "It makes you a regular person, Tessa Crimson. You can't be spot-on all the time. You made a mistake. Aiden will get over it."

She refolded the bandage and applied pressure. She was too good to me, but she was wrong. Aiden would never forgive me. I saw it in his eyes tonight.

"I don't deserve you," I said, feeling it was true. "I don't deserve to be a Smitten Kitten."

Kira squeaked and touched her chest. "Are you kidding?" She stood up in front of me and tilted her head. "Last year when I was dating all those football players, who told me that I was more than a piece of tail?"

I looked at her. "I did."

Kira glanced around the room, not seeming to care that people were watching her. "And who saved Leona from that Kitten fight at the pool with Lucy McGill after Leona called her fat?"

"Me."

"Who told Izzie that being adopted was better than having regular parents because it meant they'd handpicked her?"

I nodded. I saw what Kira was doing, but it wouldn't help. I had guilt so deep in my skin that I didn't know if I could ever perk up.

Kira leaned down, putting her hands on either side of my chair. She got close to my face. "And who"—her eyes began to water— "was there for me when my dad left?"

I sniffled. "Me."

"And that's because you're a great person. You're the queen bee for a reason."

I nearly burst into tears as I reached out and hugged her. The smell of her strawberry shampoo filled my nose and set me at ease. I could always count on Kira.

"Tessa Crimson," a nurse called from the triage room. I turned to her and then nodded at Kira.

"Thanks, K," I said, pulling back. I was glad that I still had someone.

"No prob, Tess. Just remember, a Smitten Kitten always lands on her feet." She took my arm and helped me up, then followed me to the cubicle.

Despite being a game day, Friday was easily the second-worst day of my life. I had a Band-Aid on the side of my forehead, which was not at all cute. It wasn't even pink. *And* I had a bruise on my jaw from where Chloe had punched me. Plus Christian the Creep had come to school, and Aiden was completely avoiding me. Like completely.

The one bright spot was that when I saw Chloe, she had a black eye and a small scratch on her cheek. It made me feel a little better.

The Smitten Kittens were all on edge, watching the crowds, keeping our ears to the ground. Christian would surely tell the school. If not, his sister wouldn't miss the chance. But none of the guys did more than their usual gawking. No one even seemed to have heard about Aiden and me.

"I feel like we're in the nose of the storm," Kira leaned over to whisper to me during history class. "It's eerie."

"I think you mean the *eye* of the storm." I took out my pen and drew hearts on my notebook, not looking at her. I was a mess. There was a purple, stitched welt on my forehead, my cheer skirt was wrinkled, and the paint on my toenails was chipped off. I hadn't even bothered to tie my hair up. I was a poor excuse for a captain.

Kira sighed. "Tessa," she said. "It'll be okay. Aiden is still whipped cream; I know it."

I shook my head. "He hates me."

"Cut up the charge card because I'm not buying it," she said, tickling my nose with the purple pom-pom on her pen.

Mr. Powell cleared his throat, and I glanced up at him in front of the class. I wondered if he knew—if my teacher somehow knew that my boyfriend had kicked me out of his room. But I was being paranoid.

I dropped my eyes and continued to draw on my notebook. Since I'd left Aiden's last night, I'd become numb. Well, except for my forehead, which still throbbed.

Kira looked over her shoulder toward the back of the room and then leaned into me. "Do you think Christian is going to tell everyone about SOS?"

Her voice was shaky. I didn't blame her for being nervous. Kira still cared about her social life, and she still wanted to date. If we were outed, both of those things would be crushed. But I didn't give a rusty nail. At least about dating.

"I don't know if he'll tell," I said, my voice low. "But Chloe probably will."

Kira gasped. "She knows?"

"Ladies," Mr. Powell interrupted. "Do you mind?"

Kira and I both looked up at him. "Sorry," Kira said and smiled. I closed my eyes and took a deep breath. I was completely and utterly without spirit. I just wanted class to be over. There was a slim chance Aiden would be at my locker, and there was an even slimmer chance that he might talk to me. After all, my mother had forgiven my father. Couldn't Aiden forgive me?

After history, I had left Kira to walk the opposite way down the hall when someone touched my elbow. I swung around, startled.

"What the flip?" I said. It was Christian, looking haggard, exhausted. Jingle bells! This kid was hard to shake. "Please don't talk to me," I mumbled, turning away from him. I started walking again and he fell in step next to me.

"I want to apologize," he said. My eyes felt heavy. So did my heart.

"Not accepted."

"Tessa, please," Christian said, grabbing my arm and swinging me around. I gasped. He was still not allowed to touch me.

"Get your hands off of me," I hissed, trying to pull my arm away.

His face twisted, but instead of backing up, he yanked me closer. "But . . . you kissed me back, Tessa. You kissed me last night."

He was desperate. The look on his face was absolutely desperate. I was nauseated by the reminder and the smell of spearmint that washed over my face. His hands had touched me yesterday. Ick. I pulled my arm out of his grip.

"Was it you?" I asked. Did I want the truth?

"Was what me?" Christian licked his lips, looking at mine. Gross! Dream on. His mouth would never touch me again.

"Did you send the text about Aiden and Chloe? Did you and your sister plan this whole thing?"

It only took a second for his cheeks to turn red. Carpal tunnel syndrome! That sneaky son of a biscuit. He'd sent a fake message. I'd been so stupid.

"Yes, but hear me out," he said, reaching to touch my hand.

"Ew, no!" I pushed him backward, and a few people turned to look at us. We were quickly drawing a crowd. "It was you! All along it was you, orchestrating everything!" I was yelling. I was yelling at school and I wasn't in the gymnasium. "I can't believe how manipulative you've been. Oh, my word!"

Christian's mouth hung open; he was probably shocked that I was screaming at him, embarrassed that everyone was watching us. But I wasn't ready to stop there.

"I'm sorry," he said quietly, self-consciously. "I just really liked you. I thought if you—"

"That's not an excuse!" I pushed him backward again. He stumbled. "I'm so sick of you right now." And I was. I looked him up and down, my purr transformed into a hiss. "I can't believe your tongue was ever in my mouth!"

The crowd collectively gasped. Well, if they didn't know about me and Aiden before, they certainly did now. It didn't matter. I was done with secrets.

"Stay away from me," I said in no uncertain terms. Christian looked crushed, and for a second, I felt bad about it. Like I'd broken his heart. But then I remembered how his hand had slid under my skirt as I cried. Jerk. Big stupid jerk.

I twirled around, turning my back on him, on the crowd, and I marched. I stomped down the hall and headed for Aiden's class. He'd talk to me. I wouldn't let him ignore me.

A few people whispered as I walked by. My reputation was ruined, and maybe by the end of the day, they'd know about SOS too. I turned down the English hallway and I saw him.

I saw the tousled blond hair and the long, lean body. Suddenly my urge to cry was back.

"Aiden!" I called. He stopped walking but didn't turn around. My heart sped up.

I trotted ahead, and when I reached him, I took his forearm, turning him to me. His skin was so warm. Sweet kitty princess! I missed him.

Aiden gently removed himself from my hands. "Hello, Tessa," he said looking down at me. I couldn't read his expression, but he hadn't shaved. He was sort of disheveled, and I loved him like that.

"You didn't take my calls," I said, my voice sad.

Aiden's face twitched a little, but he straightened it. "I'm sorry about that," he answered. His green eyes flicked to my Band-Aid. "I heard you needed to get stitches."

He heard? Was he asking about me? That was sweet.

"I got one," I said, trying to sound cute, the way he used to like me.

Aiden chewed on his lip, watching me, calm and collected. "Tessa," he said, dropping his eyes. "I think I need a break."

The bell rang, sending students running past us in the hallway. But Aiden and I stood there, staring at each other. It got very quiet, and I could barely breathe. "A break?"

Aiden looked down at my lips but then clenched his jaw and looked past me. I wondered if he was imagining Christian's mouth there. "I can't be with you anymore," he said. "Not after . . . everything. All the lies." He shook his head.

"But—"

"It's over. I'm sorry." He wouldn't look at me.

I didn't want to cry in the middle of the hallway, but I felt like I needed to defend myself. I wanted Aiden to understand. "We started SOS with good intentions, Aiden. They were cheating. All those guys were cheating, don't you see that?"

He snapped his green eyes to mine, pulling back his mouth in a sneer. "And you were spying, sneaking around. Why was it your business? It wasn't. You had no right."

Ouch. There was a pain growing in my chest, getting deep and heavy. "I still love you, though."

Aiden blinked and sniffled once before looking away. "Yeah, well. It's not just about you anymore."

"Don't," I said, but when I reached for him, he stepped back. Away from me.

I blinked rapidly, trying to keep the tears from spilling. I needed to go home now. My life had just been thoroughly thrashed. Aiden didn't want me. The boy didn't want me anymore.

"I'll see you around, ba . . . Tessa," he murmured.

I felt absolutely defeated. Aiden turned and slowly began to walk down the empty hall, dragging his sneakers on the linoleum. I stared after him, no longer needing to hold back my tears. Just as I closed my eyes, they leaked down my cheeks. I wasn't sure how to do this. How to properly grieve for him. Cookies and ice cream couldn't solve this problem. I wasn't sure anything could.

Christian started calling my cell, but I didn't answer. He didn't deserve that satisfaction. I deleted his messages before listening to them. I was sure that the Smitten Kittens were trying to keep SOS alive without me, especially Leona, but I'd given up all control. I'd barely been showing up for practice. I'd even missed last week's game.

Aiden didn't sit at our lunch table anymore. He sat with Darren and the team. I stared at him sometimes, but he didn't look back. He just kept his head down and chewed his food. He looked as sad as I felt.

He really was taking a break. He wouldn't take my calls. His mother had begun chatting with me on the phone, though, mostly about school stuff. She didn't ask if Aiden and I were officially over; she probably didn't need to. Obviously he didn't want to talk to me.

Christian and Chloe kept quiet about SOS. I wasn't even sure Chloe knew the whole story. But if she did, she was keeping her pouty mouth shut. Maybe she was embarrassed. Embarrassed that Aiden didn't want her. Even without me in his life, he still didn't want her scowling face.

One afternoon, I sat in the lunchroom, half dead from exhaustion. I'd been having all sorts of nightmares lately—ones where I was running around desperately, trying to finish impossible missions. The squad was with me, but my table was without pep. It was lonely.

I looked across the buzzing cafeteria at Aiden. At the same moment, he picked up his adorably blond head. His mouth opened as our eyes met, but then he dropped his gaze, staring down at his tray. Did he still love me? Did he miss me?

Right. He couldn't even look at me. I felt seriously dejected. Alone.

Kira cleared her throat from across the table. "Tess?" she asked cautiously. "We've been getting texts. Ones for SOS. But . . . things haven't been going well."

Leona snorted. I glanced at her and she widened her eyes, letting me know that Kira's words were an understatement.

"How not well?" I asked, pushing my tray away.

"Um . . ."

"Like Izzie almost got arrested not well," Leona spoke up. "And I broke my glasses." She pointed to her newly unobscured brown eyes. I was ashamed that I hadn't even noticed that she wasn't wearing her glasses. My observation skills had completely deteriorated.

Leona leaned her elbows on the table. "Without you, Tess, we're a detecting disaster. In fact"—she pointed down the table—"Kira ended up making out with the suspect! *Again!*"

I looked sharply at my friend, but she shrugged. My word. The Smitten Kittens were running wild. "Look, girls. It's time. SOS saved a lot of heartache, but at what expense?" I sounded braver than I felt. But they needed a leader. They needed me.

"He still loves you," Kira said to me, as if she knew what my real trauma was about. She smiled, her dimples deepening. "Aiden will be back."

She was a doll for saying it, but I wasn't so sure. A guy like Aiden didn't just walk around life single. Someone would get their claws into him. And they probably wouldn't make out with another boy in a car in front of his house. They'd trust him. I wished I had.

"Tess." Leona tossed a wilted fry at me. "Heads-up, Christian is on his way."

My eyes snapped up. Pork chops and applesauce! She was right. He was walking right for us—his long-sleeve T-shirt wrinkled and the bottom of his khakis shredded.

I turned quickly to look toward Aiden's table, but he was nowhere in sight. His tray was gone too. He'd left, and I was glad for that. I wouldn't want him to see Christian and me in the same room, let alone within three feet of each other.

Kira coughed as Christian reached our table. He stared down at me, his hands in the pockets of his tan pants. I couldn't even stomach looking at him. Neither could half the junior class. The rumors in the halls were that Christian had been plotting to steal me from the start. Some even claimed that Christian was a plant by the Ducks to thwart the playoffs by messing with the Wildcats' star player. I knew that wasn't the case, but I didn't bother correcting anyone. I was glad he was a social leper.

"Tessa?" he asked with his quiet voice. "Can I talk to you for a second?"

"No. You can't," Kira answered for me. I loved when she got a little attitude. It was adorable. I smiled to myself and stared down at the table, feeling slightly better.

"Fine," Christian said, sounding low. "It's for all of you anyway. I just wanted you girls to know that I'm not going to say anything about SOS. I realize that what I did was wrong. I . . ." He paused, and I wondered if he'd admit to everything he'd done. I leaned toward him.

"Look, Tessa," he said, leveling his apologetic gaze at me. "I sent that text from Cassie about Aiden, and I'm sorry."

My face became hot with anger. Leona growled from the end of the table.

Christian glanced in her direction and then back at me. "And Chloe was the one that called Aiden's mother about him drinking. She also asked the teacher to set her up as Aiden's lab partner."

"I knew it," I whispered, clenching my fists in my lap. Total scam job.

"But we didn't do it for any stupid playoffs," Christian said, his mouth pulled back in annoyance. "And Chloe didn't just do it for Aiden. She did it for me. Things have been tough for us lately and she was trying to help."

"Help herself to Tessa's boyfriend," Leona called out.

"She's not speaking to me either," he shot at Leona. "I have nothing, okay? I screwed up and I'm sorry. I just . . . I just wanted you to know that."

I didn't know whether to believe him. When he looked back at me, I could tell by his weakened eyes that he was sorry. He definitely was. There was a small tug in my chest because it was hard to watch someone standing so awkwardly. I turned away from him.

"Okay, thanks. *Bye*," Leona said. She wasn't one to feel sorry for people, but that was okay. My girls had my back. I should have told them about what I was planning to do with Aiden. They would have set me straight.

Christian stood for a minute, but I didn't look up until I heard his sandals shuffle away. He didn't stay in the lunchroom; instead, he just walked out. I felt bad for him, really. But I wouldn't talk to him again, not after everything he'd done.

"He's still cute," Kira said, twisting her gum around her finger. I looked over at her in disbelief. "What?" she asked, widening her eyes. "He is."

Christian didn't give up easily. He practically stalked me—again. Calling, waiting for me after class. It was all I could do to not speak to him. That was how I decided to handle it. I would never speak to him again. Mature? Not entirely. But effective? Most definitely.

Unfortunately, Aiden was using the same tactic on me. No phone calls, no texts, not even a note written on the back of a homework assignment. I couldn't even figure out his schedule. He was never in the halls, and I never saw him at lunch. He was like a ghost. He didn't so much as glance at me at the games. My cheer kicks were decidedly less high.

I was happy that I didn't have to do any more spying for SOS—knowing that I'd never have to videotape another sexual act or hide under another restaurant table. Kira and Leona had said they'd handle the society, but after the mishandling of the last few missions, they'd agreed it was time to let SOS go.

Leona drafted up a final letter and let me review it before sending it out. Then we hid all of our old equipment and files in a garage at Izzie's grandparents' ranch. Even though SOS was gone, we didn't have the heart to get rid of the stuff. At least not yet.

But my perk did not return. In fact, my depression seemed to deepen. I missed several practices and my new cheers were less than inspiring.

At the games, my parents' signs became more and more colorful; probably they were trying to up my spirit, but it didn't work. I needed more than glitter and puff paint. Instead, I just watched Aiden race up and down the court, successfully ignoring me whenever I was near. My parents only asked me about him once, and I told them the entire truth. No more lies. That was my new motto. Well, that and, "Can I have whipped cream on that?" This depression had earned me about five pounds of guilt.

Chloe joined a new crowd. She and Christian seemed to patch things up when he started sitting with her again at lunch. Her group consisted of other sophomores who weren't nearly as moody as her. I hoped they could give her some guidance in the attitude department. She definitely needed it.

But the Wildcats played well. Our team had made the playoffs for the first time in three years, and as Smitten Kittens captain, that should have made me ecstatic. But it didn't. It had been four weeks, and my ex-boyfriend had yet to speak to me. There was nothing inspiring in that.

I wasn't sure I'd even be able to lead the cheers for the big game. I wasn't sure of anything anymore.

SOS
TERMINATION OF SERVICES

Dear Clients,

It is with a heavy heart that SOS announces the termination of our cheater identification services. Due to recent events and dramas, it was determined that SOS was no longer able to effectively conduct investigations.

Enclosed you will find a self-discovery questionnaire to help you decide for yourself whether or not unfaithfulness is occurring. But SOS urges you to always base your decisions on concrete evidence. Not hunches. And certainly not the hunches of boys that may have ulterior motives.

SOS is thankful for your years of referrals and donations. We hope that we have made high school a safer place for your hearts.

Best of luck to you all in your future romantic endeavors.

Keep smiling,

SOS
Text: 555-0101
Exposing Cheaters for Over Two Years

CHAPTER SEVENTEEN

"IF IT MAKES YOU FEEL BETTER, TESS, AIDEN looks like total crap." Kira smiled in a show of support. The gym was loud around us as the Wildcats raced from one end of the court to the other during the final round of the playoffs. But Aiden seemed exhausted, dribbling the ball with little oomph.

Luckily for Kira, my requirement for clean language had been relaxed over the weeks. In fact, every image-conscious thing I'd ever worried about seemed absolutely petty and ridiculous. I didn't even wear ribbons anymore.

Cheering through the playoffs had been difficult. Good thing this was the last game. My self-esteem was in the gutter. I was a horrible role model, and worse yet, I was a cheater. Of sorts. I mean, sure, I'd been manipulated, but nothing excused the fact that my passion pink lips were on the mouth of someone other than my boyfriend. I'd even used my tongue. Gross.

I dropped my head, staring down at the shiny wood of the gymnasium floor. My pom-poms hung lifelessly at my side. There was no cheer that could help me now.

The shrill sound of the buzzer startled me. I felt the girls line up, poised to tell the Wildcats to attack, but I stared at Aiden. His hands were on his hips as he talked to Coach Taylor, nodding. He looked so cute in his basketball shorts. I remembered how much I always liked him after a game. All sweaty and manly. We weren't as perfect as I'd thought, but we'd been happy. I knew that.

Why had I been so quick to think he was cheating? My suspicion had gone from zero to sixty in a nanosecond. Sure, there was SOS and the history of cheaters, but Aiden didn't have a history. Maybe we really had simply grown apart. I sniffled.

I'd never brush his damp hair away from his face again. Or hear his tender whispers in my ear as he massaged my shoulders. I'd totally effed up. My life was a mess.

"Tess," Kira called, smacking my shoulder with a gray and maroon pom-pom.

Right. The buzzer had sounded, signaling that warm-ups were over. I was supposed to lead an encouraging cheer. I closed my eyes and took a steadying breath.

I was still a Smitten Kitten. People depended on me.

There was a distinct squeak as my sneakered toes crossed the planks to the middle of the court. It was soon followed by the sound of eight other squeaks. I looked at the crowd. They were pumped. People had actually painted their faces to look like cats. Normally, that would have made me smile. But now, I could only force a grin.

I lifted my maroon and gray pom-poms in the air and shook them. The room quieted at the familiar swooshing I provided. I knew the usual cheer, but it didn't seem to fit the mood I was in. Something about being miserable made me less perky. Then I began a stomp, soon to be joined by my squad.

"Get the ball, get, get the ball."

They echoed.

"Ducks will fall, yes, yes, they'll fall."

Echoed again.

"Score it, dunk it, BEAT THOSE DUCKS!"

"Let's show them, WE DON'T GIVE A FUCK!"

The crowd finished the sentence with me and then went wild with crazy screams and uproarious laughter. Well, that pumped them up. I dropped my pom-poms to my side and turned. The girls stared at me, mouths agape. The opposing team looked at me, almost frightened by the frenzy I'd created. And then the Wildcats looked at me, mostly impressed. Except Aiden. He stared at me with a look of surprise I'd never seen. He'd been so obnoxiously calm. It was nice to see that I could still ruffle his fur.

My sneakers let off an admittedly adorable perky sound as I marched back over to the sidelines. The crowd was chanting, "Sex Kittens!" They should have probably been saying, "Wildcats!" or even, "Smitten Kittens!" But what the hay, at least they were making noise.

I dropped crossed-legged on the floor and folded my hands delicately on my lap. My squad walked over, watching me like they were afraid I might pull out a switchblade and murder them at any second. I was not unaware that they all sat at least three feet from me.

The players took the court, some laughing. Aiden shot a glance over to me, still wide-eyed. I almost smiled at him, but he looked away before I could. The plump ref stood in between Dwayne and a Duck. I was mildly amused that the opposing player actually resembled his mascot. Ducks were so lame.

The room hushed. The ref tossed the ball into the air and both boys jumped. Dwayne was the first to touch it, knocking it toward Aiden. Aiden snatched it out of the air and pulled it down. He began dribbling it toward the basket, then stopped, standing at the outside of the key. Coach Taylor screamed out a play. Aiden continued to dribble and nodded at him. He passed the ball to the center, who in turn attempted a layup. It bounced off the rim into the hand of a Duck, and the teams raced down to the other end of the court.

Aiden was slow. Watching him now, I realized how right Kira was. He looked like a pile of sugar cubes. His shirt wasn't even tucked in.

The next twenty-four minutes were a slaughter. The Wildcats only scored twelve points. The Ducks had scored forty-eight. When the halftime buzzer finally sounded, the entire gymnasium let out a sigh of relief. There was only so much pain a group of overeager spectators could take.

"Tessa?" Kira approached me slowly. Her blue eyes watched me cautiously.

"Yes?"

"Um. Did you have a specific cheer in mind for halftime?" She looked frightened. I realized she'd never heard me cuss before. It must have made me look pretty hard core.

"K . . ." I paused and looked at the rest of the squad. They'd lost faith in me. I'd been a total downer for weeks and, as a result, the Smitten Kittens had lost their purr. SOS was dead. There was only one thing to do. Step aside. "You lead them," I told Kira, lifting my chin to her.

She gasped. Then the rest of the squad gasped. Well, except Leona. She said something closer to, "You have *got* to be kidding me."

Kira began to tear up and I smiled. She deserved this moment. She'd been loyal all this time. She'd been cheated on, lost out on Christian, and yet—she'd never let it affect her cheering. She should lead the big game.

"Really?" she choked.

"Yeah. *Really?*" Leona asked, unnerved.

"Kira is your lead today," I announced, sounding brave. "Make me proud, girls. I'm sitting this one out."

They looked me over sympathetically. I was one sad Kitty. They could see I needed a rest. With a quick embrace, Kira thanked me and jogged out enthusiastically into center court as the players filtered into the locker room.

The squad began a spirit-inspiring cheer about making a comeback, and I took my spot on the gym floor sideline. I picked at the shiny gray material of the pom-pom. Maybe I'd just go home. I glanced up into the crowd and saw my parents waving at me. They were so sweet.

Then out of the corner of my eye, I saw Aiden's mom. We looked at each other, and I totally expected her to gloat in some way. Instead, she raised her hand in greeting, giving me a small smile—almost like she was happy to see me. Stunned, I smiled back politely and then turned to look down into my lap. That was very strange. Quite odd.

Truth was, there was no reason for me to be here anymore. In fact, I was surely the reason Aiden was messing up. He was probably wishing I were gone. He'd never forgive me, let alone speak to me.

I was just about to stand up when I felt a hand on my shoulder. I twirled on my butt and came face to crotch with Christian. My lip curled.

"Sorry," he said and took a step back. "I know you don't want to see me."

"You're right. I don't."

"I just want to talk to you."

I pursed my lips. Yuck. I couldn't believe I fell for his lies. I couldn't believe I knew what he tasted like.

"I'm sorry I kissed you," he said, standing and looking down at me.

That was surprising. I hadn't expected him to say that. "You are?"

"Yeah." He nodded. "You were upset. I sort of took advantage of that. It wasn't right. I just really liked you, Tessa. I just wanted a chance."

He meant it. His face was obvious in its admiration. And suddenly, I kind of forgave him. Oprah once said that forgiveness was the first step in healing. And even though Christian's actions were heinous and completely out of line, the boy took a chance. There was a time when I would have fought that hard for Aiden. I should have fought harder.

"Sorry," Christian mumbled.

"Thanks for your apology," I said. He met my eyes and grinned, a glimmer of hope sparkling there. "But." I held up a finger at him. "I still think you're a jerk, and I'm still not interested. Clear?"

His smile faltered. "Crystal."

I sat and he stood, and we looked at each other. The sounds in the gym were relatively quiet. Our team was getting the stuffing beat out of them; that generally cramped school spirit. I could hear Kira's voice shouting chants, but Christian took a step toward me. I felt immediate panic as I realized that he was going to embrace me. Wait. He wanted a hug? Had he lost his marbles?

A roar rose from the crowd behind him and I looked up into the stands. The fans were cheering and pointing toward the court. I turned slowly, wondering if Kira's cheer had gone terribly wrong. Instead, I saw Aiden, stalking out of the locker room and crossing center court.

My eyebrows pulled together. What was he doing? Why wasn't

he involved in the coach's halftime talk? As he got closer, Kira's voice trailed off as she watched him stomp past the cheer squad.

Oh. My. Word. He was walking toward me. I was still cross-legged on the floor, with my lip-locking mistake hovering over me.

Aiden's face was red. Holy snapdragon! The boy looked angry, He looked . . .

"Damn," Christian mumbled.

I flipped my head back to look at him just as a fist connected with his jaw in a loud thwack. I screamed, my eyes following the length of the tan arm that was attached to Aiden's body.

Christian stumbled backward, landing in the laps of a stunned front-row fan fest. The crowd erupted in cheers. Did they think this was a stunt? Part of the halftime show? Or were they just happy to watch Christian get hit?

Wait. Aiden just punched someone in the face. He totally just hit someone without provocation. I got to my knees, beginning to scramble up to sort out the situation.

Suddenly, Aiden took me by the elbow and pulled me to my feet.

"What—"

"Zip it, Tess," Aiden said as he tugged me toward the locker room. And although I appreciated him defending my honor . . . or his, I was not about to be yanked across the court. I pulled my arm out of his grasp and swung to face him.

The Smitten Kittens parted around us, leaving Aiden and I sneaker to sneaker in center court. The crowd quieted. I was only mildly aware that we had become the halftime entertainment.

"You . . . punched someone back there," I said to Aiden as he panted in front of me. It was all I could think of to say.

"I know."

"Um . . . You're supposed to be in the locker room. Your team is losing."

"I know that too." Aiden glanced back over to the bleachers, to where Christian was holding his jaw, watching us. "You want to go help your boyfriend?" he asked loudly.

I narrowed my eyes. "No. I'm glad you punched him," I said back, motioning my hand to Christian. The crowd snickered. The acoustics in here were amazing. I hadn't even been projecting.

"Really?" Aiden put his hands on his hips. "What? Did you two break up or something?"

"Sick! I was never with him in the first place. It was a mistake, Aiden. He tricked me. He told me you were cheating on me or at least implied it." Okay, so I jumped to the conclusion on my own, but Christian had set the fur ball in motion.

Aiden seemed to consider this. He stepped closer to me, using the back of his palm to wipe the sweat off his forehead. "You weren't dating him?"

I shook my head. "No. Never."

Aiden adjusted the waistband of his basketball shorts as he looked over at the crowd. Then he turned back to me. "You should have told me everything," he whispered. "Even about SOS."

"I wish I had."

"I would have told you to stop. . . ." he added with a smirk.

"I wouldn't have listened."

"Yeah. I know you wouldn't have." He smiled. "But I'm sure we would've worked it out somehow. An arm-wrestling match, maybe."

I laughed. "Maybe."

Aiden's grin faded as he watched me. "You lied to me, Tess," he said seriously. "You lied *a lot*."

There were murmurings in the audience, and I wondered if they could hear everything, hear how sorry I was.

"I never meant to hurt you." And I hadn't. I would take it all back in a heartbeat.

He nodded, staring at me as I began to chew on my lip. At least he was talking to me. That was progress, and I should have been ecstatic. But I could smell his perspiration, and I felt the tingles that came along with being this close to him.

I still wanted him. I belonged with him. But I'd betrayed him, and I wasn't sure I would ever forgive myself for that.

I looked over my shoulder into the bleachers. My mother was sitting there with the Wildcats sign in her lap and her hand over her mouth. My father leaned forward, his elbows resting on his knees as he watched us. When he saw me notice him, he waved. Then I looked to Aiden's mom, almost expecting her to be holding a "So Long, Tessa" sign, but she looked supportively down at us. Maybe things had changed.

Aiden touched my elbow, drawing me to him. "Tessa." He paused. "I forgive you." When I looked at him, his beautiful green eyes were glassy.

"You do?" My breath came out in jagged gasps. He nodded.

"But . . ."

My heart sank.

He looked me over. "I don't know if we can fix this. I'm . . . hurt, baby. I'm so hurt."

I wanted to make it better, rewind time and erase what I'd done. But all I could do was try to smile.

He reached out to hold my cheek. "You're always so brave," he said adoringly. "Always smiling for me."

"Because you make me happy," I choked out, not wanting him to leave me.

Aiden sniffled, a tear running down his already-glistening cheek. "And you're my little ray of sunshine," he whispered.

I wanted to plead, but I didn't. Because I knew that we needed time to figure things out if we hoped to figure them out at all. This was my chance to find out just who the heck I really was, because I wasn't sure anymore. I'd been a Smitten Kitten, an SOS operative, a perfect daughter, and Aiden's girlfriend. But now I needed to find me.

"You're right," I said finally. "I think more time apart is a good idea." And it broke my heart to say it.

Aiden closed his eyes, his nostrils flaring as he stood in front of me, breathing and hanging his head. There were a couple of calls from the audience—things like: "Kiss her" and "Get back to the game." It was nice of them to care. Aiden and I had been perfect together. Or almost perfect.

Aiden opened his eyes. "You're my girl, Tessa Crimson. You'll always be my girl." He brought me close to him and wrapped me up in his arms, staring down into my face. "And even if we aren't together, that won't change."

"We could be the happiest *undating* couple ever." I smiled at him.

He laughed. "Something like that."

Someone began a slow clap. I looked over to see my dad standing, slapping his hands together loudly. My mother stood up next to him and joined in. Soon the entire gymnasium was cheering for us, applauding the saddest breakup in the history of breakups. And yet I knew it'd be okay. Even apart, Aiden and I could still love each other.

"Hey." Aiden leaned close, grinning, looking sideways at the bleachers. "Give me a kiss," he whispered. "You know, for the crowd."

I'd kiss him, all right. I'd kiss him good and plenty.

I licked my more-than-eager lips and got up on my tiptoes to press them to his. I was so happy that he'd touch my mouth again that I balled his jersey up in my hand and pulled him closer to me. Aiden and I made out—right there in center court. As the halftime show.

The crowd erupted. It was so loud that I had to reach up and cover my ears. Aiden chuckled and released me, giving the crowd a double thumbs-up. Then he turned back to me.

"You are definitely a Sex Kitten," Aiden said, looking me over.

I was about to correct him when he held up his finger.

"I mean *Smitten Kitten*."

"Thank you."

We watched each other amid the screaming fans as both of our smiles began to fade. "I'm gonna miss you, baby," he whispered.

I pressed my lips together to keep from crying and ruining the moment. "Not as much as I'll miss you, Wildcat."

Just then, the locker room door swung open and clanged loudly against the cement wall of the gymnasium. Coach Taylor came storming out. My heart sped up. Something told me that he might be a little PO'd at Aiden. When he got to us, he crossed his stocky arms across his chest and glared.

"What's up, Coach?" Aiden asked. He was still staring at me, looking nostalgic.

"*What's up?*" Coach Taylor looked ready to pounce. "Oh, I don't know, son. How about the fact that you walked out on my speech, attacked another student, and are making a spectacle in center court during halftime? Is that enough *up*?"

Aiden chuckled. "Am I suspended, then?" I darted a nervous glance between them.

"No," Coach Taylor said, looking into the bleachers. "Luckily for you the Ducks are winning. They're so high off their own fumes, they didn't hear a thing from the locker room. The principal was calling for your removal, but I talked him into suspending you from school starting tomorrow," he said gruffly, pulling up on and adjusting the waistband on his khakis. "You think I'm gonna let my star player get kicked out of the finals?"

Glad his priorities were in order. The playoffs came first.

"Tessa?" Coach Taylor asked, and looked at me. "Do you mind if Aiden fulfills his commitment to his team?" He was being sarcastic.

"No, sir."

Aiden reached over to touch my fingers. "Go cheer for me, baby," he said, leaning quickly to kiss my cheek. Then he walked over to slap his coach on the back. "Well, then, let's go!" he said wide-eyed, like Coach Taylor was the one slowing them up.

Coach Taylor exhaled as if he'd been worried that Aiden was a lost cause. He followed my ex-boyfriend as they jogged toward the lockers. Aiden turned back once to wave at me, and I giggled. He was so dang cute.

Kira stared at me as I approached the sidelines. Her face was unreadable. I paused in front of her, reaching down to pick up my pom-poms. The rest of the girls were cheering from the line, but Kira watched me. I looked behind us at the crowd, happy to see that Christian was gone. My father winked at me from behind his glasses. He was purely peachy.

"So," Kira said, slapping my hip with her pom-pom. "What was up with the make-out session? You two still broken up and shit?"

"Kira. Language."

She beamed. "Welcome back, Tess. The Smitten Kittens have missed the snot out of you." Clever girl. She'd been testing me.

I wrapped my pom-pomed hands around her and gave her a hug. She was a great friend and—for the rest of the season—captain. Even though the season ended tonight.

"All right," I announced as I pulled back. "Let's win this game with our school spirit."

She jumped up and down. The rest of the girls keyed into our enthusiasm, and the squad was in full effect. Even Leona was smiling.

Twenty minutes and fifteen cheers later, the Wildcats lost by three points. It was disappointing, but I was pretty sure that Aiden and I were both still in good moods. As his coach shook his head on the sideline, Aiden kept looking over at me and waving. He was whipped cream, even if he didn't belong to me anymore.

I'd take some time, reevaluate my goals. Maybe think up some new cheers. And then, who knew what would happen.

There would always be time for Aiden. After all, Kittens had nine lives.

SOS
UNDER NEW MANAGEMENT

Dear Clients,

I'm happy to announce the reforming of SOS. Due to a change in leadership, services were temporarily put on hold. But now we're back and totally badass.

If your boyfriend is acting suspicious, text a cheater request form to our new number at 555-1863 but be specific. For us to catch him in the act, we'll need to know exactly who he's doing.

Again, we're psyched to help out the girls of Washington High in their quest for a decent boyfriend. We're currently updating our Naughty List roster, so text with any important information.

There is now a fee schedule for our services, but for the grand reopening, we'll offer a 50 percent discount to the first ten clients.

We're back. And we're going to kick cheating ass.

SOS-XOXO
SOS
Text: 555-0101
Exposing Cheaters for Over Three Years

ACKNOWLEDGEMENTS:

Before I dive in, I figured I'd throw out a disclaimer so that a bunch of you can stop reading right now. **This story is fictional. No ex-boyfriends (or their reputations) were harmed in the writing of this novel.** Glad I got that out of the way.

First things first, I'd like to thank Ben Schrank over at Razorbill for being a smart, brave and overall awesome person. You rock! Next, I'd like to thank all of the lovely people at Razorbill, especially Anne Heltzel—a seriously butt kickin' editor—and Lexa Hillyer. And to the wonderful Laura Schechter, thank you.

My agent Melissa Sarver is an angel—patient and wise. Thank you for taking my calls. All six thousand of them.

Of course, I never would have gotten to the great people at Penguin if it weren't for my insanely cool friends and writing partners who helped me on this book. Don't fight. I love you all equally. Heather Hansen, Trish Doller, Amanda K. Morgan, Jay Asher, Andrew Carmichael, Sasha Vivelo, Daisy Whitney, Courtney Summers, the Crazy Cats over at Random Musings, and the wonderful professionals on Verla Kay's Blue Boards.

My family has always been a motivating force in my life—my grandparents most of all. But I'd also like to extend my love and thanks to my mother, Connie. Mom, you always said I was a "go-getter"! Also, thank you to my father, David Ciccone; my brothers, David and Jason; sisters, Natalie and Alex. Plus Jeff, my cousins, aunts, uncles and nieces and nephews—too many to name.

There were also some wonderfully encouraging friends and family that I'd love to give a special shout out to: Emily H., Lynny W., Richard R., Amy C., Becky D., and Brandi C. Also, a professional thanks to Andrew Karre and Amy Tipton.

Most of all, I want to thank my husband, Jesse, for always believing in this near-impossible dream. It was your encouragement and never-ending bad jokes that kept me going. And to my beautiful children, Joseph and Sophia, I promise to make dinner again sometime soon.

I hope you all enjoy the book you've helped create.